A FANTASY NOVEL THAT GETS STRAIGHT TO THE POINT: AN UTTERLY RIDICULOUS JOURNEY

JAMES TYLER BALL

© Copyright, James Tyler Ball 2023

All characters and situations in this book are fictional.

ISBN: 9798852579256

Contact
Social Media: @jamestylerball
Email: james-tyler-ball@atimetobrew.org

Books by James Tyler Ball

Fiction

Matita: The Tragic Tale of a Writer's Pencil

A Fantasy Novel That Gets Straight to the Point: An Utterly Ridiculous Journey

-

Non-Fiction

Don't Hold Your Breath: The Air-Headed World of Breatharianism

A Book About Tea: The Ultimate Graphic Guide to Over 50 Loose Leaf Teas

CHAPTER 1

Fancy a pint?

Me too. And for that, you're in the right place. Obviously, if you're in a situation in which drinking a hearty pint of mead would be inappropriate—driving, minding the kids, solving a challenging math equation—you shouldn't have a pint. But if you find yourself between the same four walls as where our story (technically) begins, you may allow yourself a playful sip of the suds.

We, my dearest fellows, are Here.

Here being a small tavern in the equally as spatially-challenged town of *Journey's End*. Confusingly, however, we are at the very start of our journey, though it will later be revealed that this is not, in fact, the beginning of our protagonist's adventure nor the end. In other words, one could say that we're over *There*, but *There* is known for a terribly poor quality of customer care, and every so often, a warbling rat is found afloat in their ale.

Perhaps *Journey's End* is not an apt name for this secluded settlement that sits fifteen miles east of *The Bastion of Beer*, nor is *Here* a fitting name for a tavern that should be over *There*.

Nevertheless, we should dilly-dally no further as the putrid stench of an open fire radiates through the tavern, infecting its food with a foul taste and dulling the sharp nip of beer, wines, and spirits.

The smoke loudly makes its way past the flickering candles on each table, the rowdy *free swords* giggle over the maiden's bosom, and the tiny tavern mice wait to be caught.

Cunningly and crucially and acridly, the smoke slips through the awkward helm of *Ser Bubbles of Beer*, who sits in a quiet corner, attempting to sip his beverage.

Doink.

Ser Bubbles' helmet gets in the way.

"Traveller?" asks the tavern maiden in a voice suspiciously similar to that of a west country local—slow, thick, and pirate-like. "Why don't you take your helmet off? You'd find drinking a much more pleasurable experience."

Beneath Ser Bubbles' helmet hops a muffled and nasally voice unbecoming of a knight of the realm. Think Richard Ayoade.

"I can't."

"What do you mean you can't?" Her bosom hangs inadvertently over the edge of his table.

"It's stuck," he explains dejectedly, whilst awkwardly eyeing the maiden's voluptuous breasts. In fact, the maiden's bosom is so enormous yet lop-sided that it causes her to walk with an unhappy spring in her step.

"How did that come to pass?" the maiden presses.

"It's a long story involving turns, twists, and an absolute lack of direction. I simply wouldn't be able to get to the point quickly enough to share it with you." If this were a film, Ser Bubbles would look directly into the camera and wink with a wry smile.

He continues, "In fact, this frustratingly rigid helmet is partly why I've come. It's a small consequence of the tumultuous goings-on fifteen miles west of here."

"You ought to choose your words more wisely, Ser. A frustratingly rigid helmet is how I fell with child, after another gentleman came." She laughs at her own joke in the way that many west-country folk do.

"Oh, haw, haw. Penis jokes? At a time like this? I'm almost offended."

"Almost?"

"Well, even I must admit this is rather a ridiculous situation I've found myself in."

"Care to explain, Ser?"

Ser Bubbles attempts another sip of his beer but can only manage a tiny drop that merely dabs his sun-scorched lips.

"Right now, there's an army of ogres plaguing my castle, *The Bastion of Beer,* ruled over by my apparently evil sister. And the only help I've got is from a snail-riding healer of the *Bon Chevaliers.* Who are, as you must have heard by now, all, probably, dead, aside from him and a few guards sent to aid me on my quest. Oh, and to make matters worse, my helmet is firmly stuck on my head, preventing me from enjoying a refreshing stein of beer. As *Ser Bubbles of Beer*, being unable to enjoy a pint is quite an inconvenience."

"Sounds troublesome, Ser."

"Just a tad."

"You're on a quest then, are you? What unexpected journey might that be?"

"No...That's *The Hobbit*." Bubbles sighs, once again looking at the imaginary camera.

"I don't follow, Ser" The tavern maiden looks on, puzzled.

"This is *An Utterly Ridiculous Journey*, not *An Unexpected Journey.* That would be the first instalment of The Hobbit. This journey is in no way associated with The Hobbit, Lord of the Rings, or J.R.R Tolkien."

"Oh, I do beg your pardon."

"However, I am looking for a band of thieves. So, I suppose there is a parallel between this ridiculous journey and that unexpected one."

"Right you are, Ser," says the tavern maiden, growing disinterested.

"Might you be of assistance?"

"Another pint?"

Ser Bubbles eyes the tavern maiden with contempt. "No. I can't even finish this one. Why would I want another pint?"

She shrugs.

"I want you to introduce me to those free swords over there."

And it's at this point in which we must leave *Here* and go over there. *There*, in this case, not being the filthy tavern with a one-star hygiene rating, but the next chapter, taking our story back a few rumbustious days.

Why might such a whirl of time, jumping back and forth, beset these pages? Because there's simply no such thing as *a fantasy novel that gets straight to the point*.

CHAPTER 2

Fifteen miles west of *Here* stands a tipsy-looking castle with thick grey walls: *The Bastion of Beer,* home to Ser Bubbles of Beer and his kin.

Outside the castle, rich farmlands of barley sway in the early evening wind, carrying a scent of drunken disasters to come. Happy village folk potter about their small town, trading eggs for hens, never to find the answer to which came first.

These are an intoxicated people who rely on the boozy fruit of Beer's farmland and the economic savvy of its lords. How anyone manages to get anything done in such a settlement, where beer flows in place of water, is a mystery as great as Machu Picchu, The Sphinx, Stonehenge, or the terrible fate of Game of Thrones season eight.

As these blitzed townsfolk pass by the castle walls, they often stop, look up and wonder, *what's the Grand Lord of Beer and his sons up to tonight?* Just like how you or I might consider the goings-on of neighbours, asking, *do they really exist or is everyone else a figment of my imagination?*

Unlike the curiously blasted townsfolk, you, dear reader, have the power to see beyond the slightly wonky castle walls and entertain the events unravelling inside.

Around a large oak table in the grand feasting hall sits our protagonist, Ser Bubbles of Beer, with a large stein in hand. The grand feasting hall is a lively place embellished with yellow and red streamers, candles encased in stain-glass fixtures, automatically playing lutes and lyres, and a few putrid piles of sick from previous nights.

Bubbles sips, sways, and laughs and would definitely be refused entry to Clubland by its brutish bouncers only a tipple up the road from Journeys End.

With him sits his useless older brother and heir to Beer, Ser Hops; his decrepit and grey old father, the Grand Lord of Beer; and the eldest of Bubbles' siblings, his sister, the ravishing but sour-lipped Little Lady Alesing, famed for her flowing auburn hair. Together the family dress in their yellow evening robes, adorned with the seal of Beer—a clump of golden barely—heartily drinking their way through the night, conversing and joking.

"My sons and lady daughter…*belch*…I can't tell you how contented it makes me to have you all here with me tonight," the Grand Lord of Beer announces with a slur.

"He always gets sentimental and soppy when he's drunk," Ser Hops says with a teasing glance at his siblings.

The Grand Lord continues, swaying as he stands, "I'm so delighted. So much so that I'd like to whip out something interesting…."

"Oh, Father, keep it in your pants!" Lady Alesing sighs with a wry smile.

"Do you remember when he started pulling his trousers down in The King's throne room at the coronation, claiming he had a joke for the queen?" Ser Bubbles asks, making his siblings roar with laughter.

"Enough of that, you swines. I'm not going to get my meat and two veg out. No." He stops and slowly smacks his lips. "Guards! Bring the special brew."

With a clap of the grand lord's hands, the feast hall guards scurry off to retrieve a barrel of Beer's special brew.

"Special brew?" Bubbles wonders.

"Indeed. I had it made especially for a special occasion...*belch,*" his father replies.

"And what occasion is this?"

"Occasion?" the grand lord pauses momentarily, raising an eyebrow and his finger to his lip as he ponders this challenging question.

"Family! I haven't been this drunk with you all in what feels like a lifetime. You, my youngest, I have missed you on your travels across our King's vast kingdom, The Land of Linear. You, my heir, what a fine lord you'll make. And daughter...if only you had a cock, you'd make a better heir than he." The grand lord sputters a cough and belly laughs so hard that the table rumbles with humour.

Only, Little Lady Alesing isn't laughing. She looks down at her hands, irked by her father's comments. *I would make a great ruler,* she thinks to herself bitterly. *I will be a great ruler. They'll see.*

With that thought, her gaze is broken as a keg of Beer's finest special brew is slammed down on the table.

"What is this special brew, Father?" asks Ser Hops.

The Grand Lord of Beer fills a cup from the keg and takes a careful sip. His eyes widen, and he coughs up a storm.

"Could be IPA. Could be APA. Could be a lager. I don't know. I was celebrating something else when I brewed it. Either way, it'll blow your sorry heads off."

Ser Bubbles reaches his cup over to get his fill, but his father lightly slaps his hand away. "No. A special drink calls for a special drinking vessel. Bubbles, fetch *The Holy Stein O' Kin Beer.*"

Bubbles and Hops look at one another with surprise, a spark in their eyes. Lady Alesing smiles politely as Bubbles fuddles his way out of his chair and exits the great hall.

Outside the hall, Ser Bubbles stumbles along the hallway, stepping over inebriated soldiers passed out on the floor. The entire hallway rumbles with a low hum of drunken snores. The only two guards still awake and remotely sober stand outside the throne room door wearing heavy mail and leather, protecting what lies inside.

The guards slouch tiredly, still hungover from the previous night's festivities. They lean on their long battle axes, holding themselves up, but as Ser Bubbles stumbles toward them, they straighten up as if they were never slacking.

"I see you. Sleeping on the job, aye boys?" Bubbles slurs.

"Not at all, my lord," one guard says.

Bubbles chuckles, "Not to worry. I don't envy you, friends."

"'Tis a great honour, my lord, to guard the grand lord's throne room," the other guard proudly booms, though his respectable air is ruined by the untimely slip of a yawn.

"Keep up the good work, boys."

Ser Bubbles nods at the guards and potters on into the throne room.

A FANTASY NOVEL THAT GETS STRAIGHT TO THE POINT

The throne room is remarkably regal and tidy for a household concerned primarily with the sordid delights of heavy drinking. Golden sapphires line the yellow woollen carpet leading up to the grand lord's throne—a mammoth seat made of the expensive wine glasses, mugs, and steins taken from Beer's enemies, loathsomely nicknamed *The Plastered Throne*. (*A Game of Thrones* would have been a very different story had this throne sat at the centre of its plot.) And lanterns lit with blue fire fuelled by a strange ethanol concoction known only to the Grand Healer of Beer furnish the surrounding walls.

But these visual delights are of no concern to Ser Bubbles. Why would they be? He sees them every day. His eyes fixate on a resplendent jewel-encrusted podium placed to the left of the grand lord's throne; on it sits *The Holy Stein O' Kin Beer.*

The Stein radiates with shimmering glass, a handle gracefully made as to rival the curves of the finest whores in Clubland, and a base fit to uphold the bountiful bosom of the Queen herself. *What a vessel*, Bubbles thinks with a cocktail of wonder and euphoria. *A cup fit for the king.*

Ser Bubbles delicately holds The Holy Stein O' Kin Beer and hugs it tightly to his chest. Dropping this revered artefact would cause massive uproar and maybe even cost his head, depending on which way the beer sways his father's mind.

You may think that is the way in which this story is headed—Bubbles drops and smashes The Stein, all hell breaks loose, maybe there's a war, a few characters you've grown emotionally attached to die, the kingdom as our protagonist knows it is turned on its head, etcetera. Alas, to your surprise, and perhaps disappointment, Ser Bubbles makes it back to the grand feasting hall without issue. (Sorry, the title of this book is an outright lie.)

As Bubbles bursts back into the grand feasting hall, his father and brother cheer with excitement; even his sister shifts in her seat out of pure reverence for The Stein he carries.

"Bubbles! Yes. Good lad. Bring The Stein to me," his father commands with a tipsy wag of his finger. Bubbles does as his father asks and places The Stein in front of him. The grand lord begins pouring the special brew into the seemingly bottomless stein.

"Sons. Daughter. Did I ever tell you the legend of *The Holy Stein O' Kin Beer?*"

"No, Father. I don't believe so," Ser Hops replies, as the guzzling of malty special brew continues.

"Well, children. This is an important lesson about your heritage…*belchhh*…It's said that when commanded by a dark soul of even darker arts, a sip from The Holy Stein O' Kin Beer turns its drinkers into greasy, fat, emerald-eyed ogres endowed with the strength of ten men." He stops pouring and takes a sip. Bubbles and Hops wait in anticipation as The grand lord freezes in place. He coughs and splutters, and with a broad smile, laughs at his sons' expectant faces who join in the boozy hysterics.

The grand lord passes The Stein to Ser Hops as he continues his story, "Legend has it that these terrifying ogres bend to the whim of whoever transforms them from human to beast."

Ser Hops passes The Stein to Ser Bubbles and asks, "And can these ogres ever be returned to man?"

"Knowledge, boy. That is knowledge of which I am uncertain. You see, my father told this story to me when I was just a boy. Only, he died of a mechanical obstruction caused by a megacolon just as he was about to unravel that part of the yarn."

"Is it not written in the libraries of Beer, Father?" questions Ser Bubbles.

"Our history was written by a bunch of confused drunks who couldn't hold a quill straight. Much wisdom has been lost to the fruit of our land," the grand lord explains ruefully.

Ser Bubbles finishes his turn with The Holy Stein O' Kin Beer and hands it back to his father, skipping his sister. She speaks up, "Bubbles! What about me?"

Her father interjects, "No, dear girl. Sipping from The Holy Stein is a rite for only the men of Beer: my heirs."

"That's ridiculous, Father. I'm the eldest. I've just as much a claim to The Stein as my brothers," she says in a growing fury.

"I'm sorry, girl. This is the way it has been for centuries. If you so wish to change the way things are, I suggest you take it up with our ancestors," the Grand Lord of Beer says sternly.

With that, Little Lady Alesing rises in frustration.

"Girl," she calls out to her serving girl, quietly standing with her head down in the shadows of the room. She is red of hair, fiery, yet meek of face. "Hold my gown, it flows too long, and I fear I may stumble," Little Lady Alesing commands.

"Goodnight, Father. Goodnight, Brothers." She nods thoughtfully, then exits the room, a heavy storm in her step.

After a few more hours of debauched guzzling, the Grand Lord of Beer finally declares, "I think we best call it a night, boys. Bubbles, take The Stein back to its rightful place."

"Yes, Father."

And so Ser Bubbles of Beer dutifully carries The Holy Stein O' Kin Beer back to its podium in the throne room, hugging it tightly all the way. He nods respectfully at the two guards on the door.

As he leaves the throne room in a drunken haze, he sees a flicker of hooded fire slinking along the hallway. Being unable to walk straight, let alone think straight, Bubbles shrugs and heedlessly heads to his bedchamber.

CHAPTER 3

A flaxen shower of morning light creeps through Ser Bubbles' bedchamber window, revealing a hulking pile of sweaty flesh in his bed. Out of his arse hangs a tiny metaphorical imp, groaning the song of the deceased and hungover.

Bubbles' naked leg hangs carelessly over the edge, the rest of his fleecy body concealed by silk sheets. He fidgets uncomfortably and lets out a beastly snore whilst a jet-black and juicy fruit-suckling fly buzzes around his head, nibbling on the oiled curls of his hair.

As Bubbles' arm flinches to swat the irksome fly away, his chamber door bursts open with a thunderous *bang*, startling Bubbles awake.

In the door stands his brother, Ser Hops of Beer, ironclad in steely battle armour, panting with apprehension.

"Bubbles! Get up," Hops frantically demands.

"What? What's going on, Brother?" Bubbles inquires as he rubs his drowsy eyes. "Why are you in your battle armour?"

The sight of Ser Hops in battle armour is an immediate cause for concern. Despite being the heir to Beer, Ser Hops has seldom seen battle, and has scarcely travelled the treacherous roads of *The Land of Linear*.

With a seriousness rarely heard in his voice, Ser Hops declares, "The Stein…It's been taken."

"Taken?" Bubbles mouth is agape. "What about the guards? They were some of our most dedicated men."

"They've disappeared. Come on, the castle's under lockdown until we find the thief."

Ser Hops races off to continue searching for the esteemed artefact, its curvaceous handle and voluminous volume sat soberly on his mind. Yet, despite the urgency of the situation, Bubbles leisurely pulls himself out of bed, weighed down by his terrifying hangover.

In the corner of his bedchamber rests his own battle armour displayed upon a wooden menaquinone. His brother might wear the steely irons of an heir, but Ser Bubbles dresses in the fierce plates of a warrior. An aureate streak runs along his chest plate, embellished at the centre by a raised clump of three barely stems—the seal of Beer. On his head, Bubbles wears a rich blond barbute helm with a T-bone-shaped hole across his face, allowing him sight and breathing space.

Once fully furnished in armour, Ser Bubbles fastens his scabbard around his waist and sheathes his flawlessly balanced sword that was forged in the hellish fires of the *MoTown-tain* volcano.

Then, swallowing his crushing hangover with a deep breath, Bubbles heads out the door, commanding his two-door guards to follow him to the throne room.

* * *

"Stay on the door," Bubbles instructs his men as he enters the throne room, finding Ser Hops investigating the scene.

"What the bloody hell is going on? Where's Father?"

"He's not yet woken, Brother. I hoped to resolve this issue before he rises," Ser Hops explains.

"What progress have you made?"

"Little. It seems after hearing of our festivities, the rest of the castle decided to join in. No one saw anything, apparently. All of our men were either fucking their whores or kissing the floor." Ser Hops sighs.

"Apart from the two men guarding the throne room," Bubbles clarifies.

"Yes. They're nowhere to be found."

Ser Bubbles eyes The Holy Stein O' Kin Beer's jewel-encrusted podium with disappointment. *Who would betray the family like this?* Sure, they spend more time drinking than governing, but the Grand Lord of Beer always made certain that the village folk had sufficient food, low taxes, and a fair rule of law. As for the castle soldiers, they were given a comfortable salary in kingly gold pieces and all the beer their hearts' desired. So, who would do such a thing? Unless...*What if someone believed the legends were true?*

"Brother," Little Lady Alesing's voice breaks Ser Bubbles transfixed gaze as she enters the room. "I heard the news. Is it true?"

"I'm afraid so."

"And Father?"

"Still asleep."

"You saw how much he drank last night. It'll be a miracle if he ever wakes up," Ser Hops interjects whilst inspecting the podium's base for clues on his hands and knees.

"I will go to him and tell of this tragedy gently. Better to hear it from his kin than a nameless guard." She nods at Bubbles and leaves the room.

Ser Hops rises, examining a single strand of ale-coloured hair on the floor. A low, bubbling groan quietly reverberates through the throne room. The brothers look at one another with suspicion.

"You've not got a bad belly, have you, Hops?"
Before Ser Hops can answer his brother's sardonic question, a towering shadow is cast over the pair. No! Two shadows, in fact, both six feet wide and six feet tall. And with another fizzling groan and a seething roar, the eye-watering stench of rotten garlic and old boiled underwear swarms Bubbles and Hops, making them retch.

It can't be…

But it is…

The legends are true…

Ogres!

Their stinging eyes widen at the sight of these two brutes, somehow adorned in the flaxen armours of Beer over their wobbling bellies and bulgingly beastly biceps. Bubbles and Hops lunge backwards, out from beneath the ogres' frigid shadows, drawing their swords and nodding at one another as if to say, *let's take these fuckers down, but what the bloody hell is going on?*

A FANTASY NOVEL THAT GETS STRAIGHT TO THE POINT

Suddenly, as Bubbles and Hops move to strike, the ogres huff and puff and let out a belch through their menacing teeth, pausing for a moment. The beasts turn to investigate an enthusiastic yet ineffective pummelling of their backs. Bubbles' guardsmen slash and hack with the determination of two Chihuahuas trying to mount a Great Dane. At this, the ogres let out a wretched roar, causing the guardsmen to stumble back and quiver under their ferocity. Then, with the power of a freight train, two hulking fists batter the guards, throwing them to the far end of the throne room.

"Brother, their weapons had no effect," Hops observes with a lump in his throat.

"To the stables, Hops. Grab as much rope as you can carry."

"And leave you here?"

"You may be the heir to the throne, but I am Beer's renowned warri—" At this very moment, a thought strikes the larger of the two ogres' obtuse brains: *turn around and stop being distracted by the dramatically dying guardsmen*. So, before Bubbles can speak the last few syllables of his hubris statement, he is walloped around in the head with an impressive thump.

"Bubbles! No!" Hops shouts with terror, holding his sword up to face the ogres.

All the whilst, Bubbles lay on the floor humming a happily delirious tune. A blow to the head does strange things to the body, and, in this case, if Bubbles weren't wearing a full-body plate of armour, we might see its effects rise from his pants. He pulls himself together.

"Go, Brother. The ropes!" he giggles. "I'll handle the beasts."

As Bubbles unsteadily gets to his feet, Ser Hops darts to the exit, propelled by his fearfully pulsating arsehole.

"Beasts! You may have stricken my head, but your power is no match for the headache caused by a festive night in Beer."

Whether Bubbles' arrogance is due to the knock to his head or the effects of his nasty hangover is unknowable. Still, all reason flies in the face of his decision to charge at the mammoth ogres.

"Arggggggghhhhhh! For Beer!" he roars.

CHAPTER 4

Little Lady Alesing approaches her father's bedchambers with her hand pushed awkwardly against her leg—a sliver of silver shines through the gaps between her fingers. She takes a deep breath and enters, not before asking his door guards to leave them a moment of privacy as she breaks the terrible news.

"Father?" she asks to no response.

The Grand Lord of Beer lies asleep feverishly, his golden bed robes steeped in sweat, experiencing the hideous effects of last night's festivities. There comes an age, some of you may know, wherein the giggle juice begins to have an overall nasty effect on one's body. Your eyes wither into dried prunes, your energy slumps like a sloth, you begin to see fairies where none exist, and, in particularly bad cases, your skin turns as yellow as ogre piss. If the Grand Lord of Beer were an ordinary human, no doubt he'd have died long ago, calcified by liver-spotted scars, but he is a man of Beer, born and bred of ale so that he may feel no ailments.

Little Lady Alesing kneels by her father's bedside. She grabs his hand and speaks softly, "Father. Wake up." The grand lord groans unresponsively. "Father?" She tries once more as he stirs, mumbling

"No…" He smacks his lips together. "No. You can't do that, Yeti." He giggles like a child. "It'll blow my coc—" Little Lady Alesing shakes her father's hand, fearing what he might say in his bemused state.

Suddenly, the grand lord flies upright, wheezing for breath. His chest rises and falls with frenetic determination as sweat pours from his chin.

"Father, are you sick?" Alesing asks with feigned concern.

"No, no, daughter. I have but a touch of the leftovers. I'm not as young as I used to be," he says with a wry smile. The grand lord coughs and sputters. "Guards! Guards, fetch my serving boy. I require water."

"I sent them away, Father."

"Why on earth would you do that? I'm parched," he wonders.

"To give us privacy, for I bring grave news." She bows her head.

"News...Of what, girl? Spit it out," he demands

"The Holy Stein O' Kin Beer is missing."

The Grand Lord of Beer pauses, uncertain of how to respond. Through a phlegmy hack, he manages, "Stolen?"

"Brother Hops is leading an investigation to find the thief. The castle is on lockdown," she explains neutrally.

With a burst of energy belittled by a pang of tremors, the grand lord asks, "Why did no one wake me? I have a mind to interrogate the villagers, the guards, anyone who's set foot in the castle in the last year!"

"We thought it best to leave you in your slumber. Hops had ideas to find it before you woke."

"Foolish boy. Still, in my ripe old age, I'm yet to teach him how to rule." He slumps, dejected, and raises a hand to tenderly cup Alesing's face. She loosens her grip on the silver concealed beneath her hand. "Dear girl, if only you were born a man, you'd make a fine ruler."

"Father," she pauses, "name me your heir instead of Hops. At least, until he is fit to rule."

"I'm sorry, girl. It cannot be done." He pauses, regarding his daughter. "Now, fetch my guards. I've a mind to find the thief myself."

Little Lady Alesing springs up from her knees, incensed. The grand lord flinches, startled by her anger.

"All my life, Father—" Tears begin to roll. "—I've been second to—no third—to Brother Hops, yet I have bested him in all disciplines of a great ruler."

"Alesing. We've discussed this before. Never in the history of *The Land of Linear* has there been a Grand Lady. It is not the way, dear girl."

"I will be the first—" She lets the words hang. "—dear Father."

Again he starts explaining why her dream may never be realised, but Little Lady Alesing stops listening. She has had enough of listening. The silver tingles in her hand, reminding her of its presence.

Little Lady Alesing furrows her brow. She raises her hand, revealing her slender dagger.

"Alesing! Stop this at once." The grand lord's face is a picture of terror, his mouth agape and his eyes so wide that one might wonder if they're stuck. "Guards!" he desperately cries. "Gua—" Little Lady Alesing brings her dagger down on his throat, ending his life in one swift swoop. With luck, she avoids her father's sputtering blood as it flows into a vivid red river, bright, unlike death. The smell of booze fills the air.

"I'm sorry, Father," Alesing mutters as she drops the blade. It lands with a menacing thud that echoes through her ears. Determination smites Little Lady Alesing's face. "Girl. Enter."

From outside the room, Alesing's serving girl enters. Her eyes are pure white and without pupils, and she speaks to her mistress in a strange language, "Oui, Mistresse. Howment puis-je aidelp?"

"Cover yourself in my father's blood, then cower in the corner of the room. Do not leave until you are collected," Alesing commands.

"Oui, Mistresse." The serving girl does as she is told whilst Alesing leaves the room screaming with feigned upset, "Guards! Oh, somebody help! Guards!"

CHAPTER 5

Slam! A pair of mammoth ogre fist strike the stone floor with a stunning crack (much like the whores of Clubland). Little rocks fly through the air in a hazy plume of dust as Ser Bubbles of Beer dives backwards, avoiding impact. Again, another set of olive anvils aim at Bubbles and smite the stone between them.

Quick on his feet, Bubbles scrapes the sharp end of his sword along the floor and engraves a thin grey line around the ogres. It creates a piercing sound that piques the beasts' interest. He swiftly swoops behind the beastly pair—the backside of an ogre is a grotesque place, plagued by putrid smells, dying flies, and junk you ain't never seen in a trunk.

Bubbles charges toward the back of the bigger ogre and jumps on its back with a soft, fleshy thud. The ogre wobbles, and like a great tree axed by a lumberjack, falls into its friend. *Clap!* Both ogres dance on one foot, waving their hulky arms around like a pair of utterly demented ballerinas. Ser Bubbles smiles at this sight, leaning on his sword.

As Bubbles enjoys the, frankly, strange show, Ser Hops rushes in with several metres of rope trailing behind him.

Out of breath, he says, "Brother, some of the horses escaped, but I got the rope."

"What? You didn't need to take the rope from the saddles!"

"You said to get some rope." Hops looks on blankly.

"Not rope that's being used, Hops." Bubbles shakes his head. "Never mind that, we haven't got much time until they get their bearings. Give me a rope. I'll go left. You go right."

As the giant spinning tops slowly twirl without grace, the brothers approach from both sides, tying their ropes into lassos.

"When I give the signal, tie your rope round its neck," Bubbles says, to a nod of acknowledgement from Hops.

The brothers spin their lassos in the air like a pair of cowboys wrangling cattle, watching the ogres sway with dizziness. As it turns out, to Bubbles' surprise, ogres spin for an unusually long time.

"Now!" Bubbles shouts.

Ser Bubbles and Ser Hops whip their ropes forward with a snap of the air. Their lassos land around the ogres' necks.

"Pull!" Bubbles commands.

With the force of their ropes wrapped tightly around their necks, the giant beasts fall onto their sides, growling with frustration.

"Quickly, Hops. Bind their hands." Bubbles cuts a length of rope with his sword and kneels beside the larger ogre, tying his hands with a trembling chatter of his teeth. Hops does the same, only the stench of his ogre is so putrid that he almost pukes up over himself.

"These ropes won't hold them for long. We'll need to take them to the dungeon," Bubbles says whilst the ogres sit upright, panting and grunting with resignation. "I'll fetch more guards." Hops sprints off and returns with a small squad of soldiers.

"Where were all of you? Don't tell me you didn't hear the commotion?" Bubbles says scoldingly.

"Well, our absence was necessary for the plot, my lord," one guard explains. "Your prowess as a warrior needed to be established."

Bubbles rolls his eyes. "Take these brutes to the dungeon. Lock them in separate cells and barricade the doors once bolted."

"Yes, my lord," the soldiers say in unison.

"And watch them closely. They're particularly strong," Bubbles warns.

The soldiers pick up the ropes, two to an ogre. They flinch at the deep rumbling noises the beasts make as they're led out of the throne room.

"Excellent work, Bubbles," Hops says, relieved.

"Yes, it must be time for a little celebration," he suggests.

"Then we'll continue our search for The Stein."

But before the brothers can leave the room and find themselves a cold goblet of Beer's finest, Little Lady Alesing rushes in, holding her dress up by the sides so as not to trip, with streams of tears rolling down her cheeks.

"Brothers…" She falls to her knees in front of them.

"Sister! What is it?" Bubbles says with concern as Hops lowers himself to hold her arm.

"It's father…" She pauses, theatrically. "He's…He's dead."

"Dead?" Bubbles whispers under his breath, momentarily losing mental lucidity as Ser Hops flushes pale with dread.

* * *

Outside the late grand lord's bedchamber, Ser Bubbles, Ser Hops, and Little Lady Alesing stand with Trappy, the Grand Healer of Beer—a grey old man with a grey old demeanour and a grey old beard flowing down to his knees. Behind them, through the doorway, the group can see the brutal scene of their father's murder, still fresh with blood and the spoilt smell of death.

"His throat is slit, my lords…and lady," the grand healer explains, despite it being obvious.

"Why would anyone do such a thing?" Ser Hops asks, anger and frustration growing in his voice. Nearby guards stare.

"Calm yourself, Brother. Despite what a terrible elixir it is to swallow, our Father's death means you will soon be crowned as grand lord. People are watching your every move," Ser Bubbles reminds his elder brother with a comforting pat on the shoulder. Hops looks down, his lower lip quivering.

"My brother does ask a good question, Grand Healer. Why?" Bubbles inquires, his eyes growing wet.

"Why is not a question I can answer. Only your father's murderer knows *why*. What I can answer is *who*."

Holding back his upset for the benefit of his siblings, Ser Bubbles looks at Ser Hops, who looks at Little Lady Alesing, who looks back at Bubbles. *Who would want to murder the Grand Lord of Beer?* Their eyes ask one another.

"Your serving girl, my lady," Grand Healer Trappy reveals with a heavy voice.

"But she was always such a loyal servant to me. It cannot be!" Alesings arms flail in a mild display of protest.

"I'm afraid she was found curled up in the corner of your father's bedchamber. The dagger used to slit his throat was only a few feet away."

"Where is she?" Ser Hops steps forwards.
"Locked in the dungeons, awaiting your judgement, my lord."

"Take us there," Hops demands.
"There is one more thing." The grand healer pauses. "She's not entirely herself."

"What do you mean, Grand Healer?" Bubbles asks, tilting his head.
"See for yourself."

The group head to the dungeons—a dark place, as to be expected, that sits on the far right side of the castle. Behind iron bars, each cell is lined with horse shit and hay. A little barred window gives prisoners a sliver of respite from the shadows and foul odour. As they enter the dungeons, they are reminded of the two ogres who punch the walls and groan like castrated lions.

"The legends are true, it would seem," Trappy says as they pass the beasts. "The Holy Stein O' Kin is missing and ogres have appeared. That means—" They approach the girl's cell. "—sorcery is afoot." The grand healer opens the cell, revealing the girl curled up in a corner, rocking back and forth.

"Bethison," the girl sharply whispers to herself, *"Bethison...Bethison..."*

"What is it she says, Healer?" Ser Hops asks.

"I'm not certain. The language she speaks is beyond my knowledge."

"Her eyes..." Bubbles looks on, his mouth agape.

"Yes. Pure white. A sign that she is under the influence of a spell," the grand healer explains.

"Is there any way we can find out what she's saying?" Little Lady Alesings wonders, hoping the answer is *no*.

The Grand Healer of Beer strokes his long beard as many wise men do whilst lost in thought. He raises a finger with inspiration, *"Bon Chevalier."*

"The snail castle?" Bubbles gasps.

"That's right. The language she speaks, it's similar to *Franglais*, tongue of the snail. The grand healer there is a knowledgeable man who dabbles in the art of magic. Perhaps he can better assess the girl than I," explains Grand Healer Trappy, stroking his beard again as if to command authority over his idea.

Ser Hops looks up, determination and pride in his eyes. He steps forward, standing straight as a crooked nail, "I shall travel to Bon Chevalier with the girl and find a way to avenge our father."

Shall I? He nervously thinks to himself.

"With all due respect, my lord. You are to be crowned grand lord of Beer. You must remain here and provide reassurance to your subjects," Trappy regrettably explains as Ser Hops' regal demeanour slumps into disappointment.

"But…I must…avenge my father!"

Phew...Ser Hops gasps in his head.

"Brother, you will be our ruler, and a fine one at that." Bubbles manages a supportive smile.

"Perhaps I could have a squad of guards escort the girl with a letter from yourself, Ser Hops," the grand healer suggests.

That same regal and honourable light that only a moment ago shone down upon Ser Hops' shoulders now shines on Ser Bubbles, "No! This girl is possessed and dangerous. She killed the grand lord! I shall go. I am Beer's most renowned warrior. I have travelled the road to Bon Chevalier before."

"My lord?" Trappy looks to Ser Hops for his approval. He nods, knowing his brother is the best man for the job.

"Then let us chain the girl. Guards!" the grand healer shouts.

CHAPTER 6

From the stables emerges Ser Bubbles of Beer, mounted on his second favourite steed, *Pearwood*, her charcoal coat shimmering under the early afternoon sun. His favourite horse, *Terry*, was found dead three weeks ago after choking on a thin slice of wet lettuce. A tragedy, a comedy, but probably for the best—who wants a warhorse that can't handle its leafy greens? Nevertheless, at the time, Bubbles was bereft (and out of salad).

Bubbles canters to the middle of the castle courtyard between the keep and the outer walls. Across the yard, Ser Hops and Little Lady Alesing stand with two guards who restrain the serving girl, still speaking in her devilish half-language. As Bubbles approaches her, his horse neighs and rears, making a fuss over her presence.

"Woah there, girl, she can't hurt you," Bubbles reassures his mount, petting her mane.

"You hope," interjects Ser Hops.

"She will be bound the entire journey by these two guardsmen. She won't cause a fuss," Bubbles explains confidently.

"Still, Ser Bubbles, you must be cautious. We do not yet know what power she holds," the grand healer warns.

"Brother, might I make a suggestion?" asks Little Lady Alesing. Bubbles nods. "Don't take these guards with you. Travel alone."

"But the path to castle *Bon Chevalier* is treacherous, lined with highwaymen, goblins, and sly foxes, my lady. No, Ser Bubbles, you must," the grand healer protests.

"Taking your guards will only draw more attention to yourself, Brother, and the girl. Once news spreads of our father's death and the loss of The Stein, you will be seen as vulnerable. These guardsmen will only make your presence more obvious," she explains.

A FANTASY NOVEL THAT GETS STRAIGHT TO THE POINT

Bubbles considers Little Lady Alesing for a moment. "Hops. What do you think? Sister says no guards, Grand Healer Trappy says otherwise. You have the deciding vote."

"Me!?" Ser Hops looks around, flustered. "Well—" He looks at his sister for guidance; *father always said she'd make a great ruler if only she had a cock*. "Alesing makes a compelling argument. Better to travel covertly and avoid confrontation than to take guards and need their swords."

"Then it is settled. I will travel with the girl alone. Guards, bind the ropes around her waist and wrists so that I might lead her—

"—like the animal she is!" Hops interrupts, trying on a new, harsher attitude as the soon-to-be crowned ruler of Beer, but both Bubbles and Alesing see that it's an uncomfortable fit. Hops notices their eyes and softens his demeanour. "You must return in time for Father's funeral and my coronation, Brother."

"Indeed I shall, though no doubt I'll be waylaid in such a way that lengthens this story and develops my character."

Ser Hops nods in agreement with an upturned smile, accepting that his younger brother is burdened by narrative.

"Brother—" Little Lady Alesing pauses dramatically. "Be careful."

Ser Bubbles smiles, puts on his golden helmet over his jet-black curly hair, and heads for the castle gates. The serving girl is tethered behind him, dragging her feet as they move. They ride off, past the gates, onto the unforgiving yet remarkable straight road spanning the length of *The Land of Linear*.

* * *

As evening falls and both the sun and moon hang in the purple sky, Little Lady Alesing retires to her bedchamber. She places two guards on the door and instructs them not to let anyone inside, not even her brother or the Grand Healer of Beer.

Inside her bedchamber sits a vanity desk laden with sapphire-encrusted brushes, bracelets, and jewellery befitting a lady. There also sits a mirror split into two sides with a deep back and two oak handles sitting on the front. Little Lady Alesing sits at her desk and brushes her auburn hair for a moment as she regards herself in the mirror.

I am the ruler of Beer now, she thinks as a sneer hangs on her face.

Little Lady Alesing leans forward, puts her brush down, and pulls open her mirror, revealing a cobalt-coloured rock adorned with a glistening transparent crystal upon its top. Though such devices are naturally forming in The Land of Linear, it just so happens that Little Lady Alesing's crystal formed in the unfortunate shape of a small shaft and two suspicious-looking balls at its base. So, though what's being described is a crystal ball, a more appropriate name for her device might be her *crystal balls*.

She waves her petite hand over her crystal balls, causing its glass to grow cloudy with magical dust and twinkle with ethereal light. Suddenly, her bedchamber turns dark, but Little Lady Alesing's face glows brightly under the blue hue emanating from her crystals.

Upon her balls, three faces appear, each with long, wart-covered noses, pink, green, and purple skin, and piercing eyes as sharp as a jester's wit. They wear pointed hats, and each holds broomsticks and black cats, and they do it all just to scare those fearful individuals who buy into the stereotypical image of a witch. Yet, these three hags that sit upon Little Lady Alesing's balls are indeed no witches. They are far worse: they are sorceresses—the elders of *The Cup 'n' Sorcerers*.

"What news do you bring us, Sister?" hisses the pink-skinned sorceress whose name is *Greed*.

"My father is dead," Alesing says with not a sliver of guilt in her voice.

"And what of your brothers?" croaks the green-skinned sorceress whose name is *Power*.

"Ser Hops remains in the castle. My younger brother, Bubbles, is travelling to *Bon Chevalier* with my serving girl, who I framed for my father's murder."

"And do you have it? *The Holy Stein O' Kin Beer?*" wheezes the purple-skinned sorceress whose name is *Beetroot*.

"Yes, sister. It is hidden here in my bedchamber."

The sorceresses cackle as all black cat-wielding individuals do. *Power* snaps her fingers, and lightning thunders triumphantly outside Alesings window. She gasps, startled.

"Sister…" *Power* starts.

"You must deal with your brother Bubbles…" *Greed* continues.

"And raise an army of ogres," *Beetroot* finishes.

"I will do as you command, great sisters," Alesing agrees.

With a white puff of smoke, the three faces disappear. Alesing swipes her hand over her crystal balls once again, revealing Ser Bubbles of Beer and the serving girl on their journey. She watches as Bubbles' horse saunters along, growing tired along the sun-scorched road. The girl stumbles behind them, her rope led by Ser Bubbles.

Though Little Lady Alesing is a strong sorceress trusted by *The Cup 'n' Sorcerers*, she is not yet powerful enough to strike a man down from afar. Up close, she might be able to throw a fireball or manifest menacing shards of ice to pierce Bubbles' heart, but from afar, she is limited. As such, she must rely on manipulating his environment.

Considering how best to murder Bubbles, Alesing watches her balls, surveying her brother's surroundings. She notices a thicket up ahead, rustling unnaturally. The road that passes through *A Really Hot Place*—a desert located at the base of *Melting Pot MoTown-tain*, a goliath volcano where all different races, beasts, and animals burn in a swirling mess of acid jazz—seldom sees a breeze strong enough to rustle a man's hair. This is due to an odd scientific lore that you probably have no desire to learn. So, we shall skip the made-up science of The Land of Linear and join Little Lady Alesing in wondering why a bush might be swaying in a place without wind.

Alesing watches as a scaley grey goblin crusader suddenly scurries out from behind the thicket.

"Traveller," the goblin creaks.

"Woah there, goblin. Surprising a man like that could get you killed," Bubbles says.

"No. For I am protected by my lord and saviour *Sour-Ron*, the all-seeing eye. You must join me in my worship." The goblin raises a crucifix.

"Sorry, I don't think it's for me. The only thing I worship is beer."

"You must!" the crusader screeches.

"No."

"Well, at least take one of these pamphlets," the missionary huffs.

"I've got no room or time for such light literature, goblin. Be on your way."

"No! No! No! I'm tired of travellers disregarding my lord Sour-Ron. If you do not join me as a follower, I will be forced to smite you with my lord's justice," the goblin growls.

"Fat chance!" Bubbles remarks. He dismounts from his horse whilst awkwardly continuing to hold the girl's rope, then he and the goblin clash into combat.

As steel hits steel and sparks fly, Bubbles is on the back foot, burdened by the serving girl. Little Lady Alesing sees an opportunity.

S'épee best gontie, Alesing whispers, forcing Bubbles' sword to sporadically fly out of his hand.

"My sword!" he shouts, stumbling backwards and falling onto the burning road. The grey goblin raises his cleaver to Bubbles' throat. He intones in a raspy south American preacher voice, "Submit to my lord now, and be rid of your sins, boy."

Bubbles frantically looks around, searching for a way out.

"Lord have mercy," the goblin says with a scowl as he raises his cleaver. Thinking quickly, Bubbles pulls his helmet off (not a euphemism) and heavily smacks it into the goblins cleaver deflecting the impending blow. Bubbles then jumps up and strikes the crusader in the chest with an ogre-like punch. The goblin drops to his knees, winded, as Bubbles grabs his sword, replaces his helmet, and climbs atop his mount, continuing his journey.

"*No!*" Little Lady Alesing gasps aloud from her bedchamber. She pauses in thought, trying to remember all the spells the sisters taught her. Her eyes widen with inspiration.

Armbaton st'armure, armbaton st'armure, armbaton st'armure, she chants.

At this, Bubbles' head grows warm, as if his helmet is cooking under the sun. He feels a tingling at the back of his head, but the feeling soon fades.

Alesing watches as Bubbles continues on unhindered. She slams her desk with frustration.

Yet, unknown to Alesing, her brother is not impervious to magic; instead, she simply said the wrong spell. The language of sorceresses is challenging, even for lifelong scholars. She should have said *ambrulure bur'armure*, which would have caused Bubbles' skin to melt under the growing heat of his armour.

Little Lady Alesing continues to watch Bubbles as he brings his steed to a halt. He reaches into his saddle bag and retrieves a leather flask presumably filled with water but probably filled with beer. Bubbles pulls at his helmet so he can more comfortably drink from his flask, yet something is amiss. Try as he might, his golden helmet, beginning to glow under the boiling sun, won't budge.

Has my head swelled so much under the heat? He wonders, pulling at his helmet once more.

Alesing can't help but chuckle at the terrible inconvenience she's caused her youngest brother, putting her in better spirits. So, as Bubbles fights with his helmet, she decides to leave him to sweat to death beneath the pummelling sun and warm weight of his headpiece. She sheathes her balls.

CHAPTER 7

Travelling along the perilously straight road of *The Land of Linear*, passing through *Joker's Canyon*—a place where nasty jibes are whispered on the wind—with an unscathed ego, sloshing through the shallow waters of *Puddle*, and springing up the rubber steps of *Bouncy Castle*, Bubbles finds himself in *A Really Hot Place*.

The sun beats down on Bubbles' stuck helmet, its gold colour glistening and growing ever redder under the heat of the desert. Sweat showers down from his neck, splashes on his armour, and evaporates into salty steam. He pants like a dog whilst sitting atop his horse.

Behind Bubbles trails the serving girl, still adorned in her dark robes, unphased by the heat. She stumbles regretfully, slowing the journey and increasing Bubbles' chances of dying from exhaustion.

"Keep up the pace, girl," Bubbles commands with a laboured breath. "We've not far to travel." He tugs at her rope.

Bubbles looks to the side of the road, up at *Melting Pot MoTown-tain*—it's a volcano like no other. There *ain't no mountain high enough* to rival the size, scale, and funky magnitude of the Melting Pot MoTown-tain.

Acid spits from the mountain's peak, hitting its side with a tight pluck of soulful bass. Literally soulful, for within the swirling pit of acid jazz swims the desperate souls of travellers and soul singers past. And as the mountain's acid chamber bubbles, it releases its victims into the melting desert atmosphere to wander aimlessly for all eternity, desperately searching for record contracts, better streaming royalties, and their riders.

Heat lines wobble as Bubbles looks onwards and the sound of MoTown-tain's music shivers past his ears. *I've been really trying, baby...*

"Do you hear what I hear, girl?" Bubbles looks around, paranoid.

The girl offers her captor no response.

Let's get it on...cluck...

Bubbles' eyes widen. "A—"

Let's get it on (ooh) (ooh)...gobble...

"—chicken?" He raises an eyebrow. Wind—that's right, wind in a place with no wind—brushes past Bubbles' helmet and rushes through its gaps, striking fear into his *soul*. From seemingly out of nowhere, this unaccountable gust is followed by the spring of a turkey adorned in gold chains and cool shades, flapping right in front of Bubbles' face.

"Jive Turkey, mutha fucka!" The turkey says with the smooth voice of Marvin Gaye.

Startled, Bubbles fumbles his sword from its sheath and points it in the Jive Turkey's beak. "What? What the hell are you?" Bubbles asks, utterly perplexed.

"I'm the Jive Turkey round these parts, Ser Bubbles," he clucks in Marvin Gaye's voice.

"Wait...How do you...How do you know who I am?" Bubbles continues holding his sword suspiciously.

"Oh, I heard it through the grapevine," the bird clucks. The serving girl looks at her captor, with his coal-red helmet and profusely sweating neck, as he aimlessly waves his sword in the air. *The desert madness is setting in,* she thinks to herself.

"Life is for learning," the turkey sings. "Some songs will show you which way to go, if only you would listen."

Bubbles tilts his sword away from the turkey with a deep sigh. "Which way?" His words begin to slur. "Which way to The Holy Stein O' Kin, turkey spirit?"

"The world is just a great big onion," the turkey flaps as a woman's voice quietly harmonises with his own.

"What does that mean, magic turkey? I wish to know the meaning of your presence," Bubbles demands, raising his sword.

"Two can make that wish come true," the turkey sings (he's not foreshadowing, just singing).

A FANTASY NOVEL THAT GETS STRAIGHT TO THE POINT

Bubbles looks down at the girl, "Two?"

As he turns toward the girl, a whirl of turkey feathers swarm through the air. *Bang!* The turkey flaps into Bubbles' helmet, disappearing into a cloud of dust, turkey feed, and musical notes. Bubbles' arms flail as he fights to retain balance on his horse's saddle. The girl tugs at her ropes, bound to the horse's backside...

Thud. Her tug pulls Bubbles from his saddle and causes him to fall to the ground, hitting his head.

Bubbles fights to keep his eyes open, but they grow heavy and delirious. A tiny turkey spins around his head, cuckooing and clucking and gobbling. And as Bubbles loses consciousness, the turkey whispers one final lyric, "It's witchcraft, wicked witchcraft."

Darkness.

* * *

It may completely shock you—or not—to learn that Ser Bubbles of Beer isn't dead. In fact, this is one of those moments in which a stroke of narrative luck saves our hero because, although this is *A Fantasy Novel That Gets Straight to the Point*, our adventure would be cut far too short if Bubbles were to die now.

Bump. Bump. Bump.

Bubbles' eyes flinch and flicker still closed. He lets out an exhausted groan, then sits up with a scream, "Jive Turkey!" His breathing is heavy as he takes in his surroundings. Bubbles processes the current events slowly, his mind tired from the turkey, soul, and desert heat.

The girl trails behind, tied to a rope, just as expected. She remains attached to Pearwood, but Pearwood trails behind, too, without Bubbles in his saddle. He blinks slowly. "What's going—" Below him sits the glossy shell of a…

"Ah, you're awake," a thick nasal accent speaks from the back of an unknown mouth, merging and slurring words.

Bubbles looks up and down through milky eyes. "What's? Who are—"

"Don't worry, mon ami. You are safe now. It seems you had a touch of the desert madness," the unknown man explains.

Bubbles eyes the smooth surface beneath him, running his hand along its groves. "This isn't a horse," he determines, befuddled.

The unknown man chuckles, "Non, traveller. It is escargot."

"It's…massive…" His eyes grow large as he lets out a startled shriek and thrashes around violently.

"Calm down, mon ami. You'll hit your head again. It won't bite. Giant snails are the transport of choice for us *Bon Chevalierians*." The man chuckles.

A Eureka moment strikes Bubbles, "Bon Chevalier? That's where I'm headed."

"Yes, I thought as much from the ancient language your prisoner speaks."

"You speak her language? You can translate?" Bubbles grows excited.

"I'm afraid not, but I recognise it as the opposite of my own. The Grand Healer of Bon Chevalier will help." He whips his snail, encouraging it to go beyond a snail's pace.

"Who are you?" Bubbles looks at the man. He is dressed in brown and beige armour made from snail shells, and he rides without a helmet, letting his hair hang just like the cigarette on his lips. His demeanour is sleepy.

"I search the desert, looking for those who've succumbed to the madness, by order of the Grand Healer of Bon Chevalier."

He flips open a satchel pegged into the side of his snail and pulls out a horn of water. He hands it to Bubbles. "Here, mon ami, drink. You must be parched."

Bubbles weakly pushes the stranger's hand away. "I can't. My helmet is stuck."

"Can you fit your tongue through the hole?"

Ser Bubbles awkwardly pokes his tongue out, his eyes crossing over one another as he looks at his mouth. "A bit."

"So lick it up like a dog," the stranger chuckles. "You will need your strength. Bon Chevalier is a strange place for outsiders."

CHAPTER 8

After journeying through *A Really Hot Place*, the relentless sun battering Bubbles, the heat finally breaks with a cool breeze as he and his travelling companions approach the glorious vineyards of Bon Chevalier. *Oh, how I'd guzzle a glass of sweet wine if not for this blasted helmet*, Bubbles thinks to himself.

Field after field of lushes viridescent hedges stretch as far as the eye can see. Above each thicket, Bubbles glimpses the bare shoulders of grape-pickers, their oily brass skin glistening with sweat.

"Are these women naked?" he asks the Chevalierian scout as his snail slithers along the path to the castle.

"Of course, mon ami. It is the best way to pick grapes—to feel the fruit of the land brush against your bosom," the Chevalierian explains, unphased by the sight.

Bubbles shakes his head, finally returning from his dazed state.

"Wait 'till you see our grand lord." The man smiles, entertained at the thought.

The snail on which Bubbles sits passes through the vineyards and a small village at the base of Bon Chevalier castle, made up of breezy tents, crude cafés, and pipe stands. Accordions and Tanbur music plays as village folk jig together, arm in arm, wine flowing.

As they close in on the castle of Bon Chevalier, Bubbles looks up in wonderment. The Bastion of Beer is a grand and regal fort, but this...Its white granite exterior, short walls made for appearance, not war, and grape red roofs sitting atop its watch towers are a sight fit for the medieval equivalent of Instagram. The King must be truly jealous of this castle; it's a surprise that he's not already commandeered it for himself.

An outrider meets the scout and his guests on another snail, much larger than the scout's, with an ice blue shell to match the colour of his armour. They speak to each other in a strange language, much like the tongue the girl speaks, only different.

"Arrétez-vous, scout," the guard commands, tugging at the reins of his snail with a firm hand held up.

Bubbles looks at the girl as the scout and castle guard talk; her head perks up, tilted, recognising the rhythm of their language. Bubbles, on the other hand, is perplexed by this muddled tongue and their thick accents.

"What's he saying?" Bubbles asks.

"Qui as-tu ici?" The guard regards Bubbles with suspicion.

"Mon ami, il est Beerian. Il est venu voir le Grand Seigneur."

"Then allow me to speak in a tongue your guest understands. What is your business here, Beerian?" the guard demands.

Bubbles swivels around from the back of the snail and clumsily dismounts, brushing the dust off his steel gauntlets, then clearing his throat. "I am not just any

Beerian. I am *Ser* Bubbles of Beer, son of the Grand Lord of Beer, Slosh the Second." He bows and politely smiles, smugly adding, "You've probably heard of my exploits."

Despite his face being covered by a menacing blue helmet, Bubbles can see the guard pull a disgusted grimace beneath. He says, "I've heard you're a drunk, just like your father."

"My father…" Bubbles contemplatively looks at his hands.

"Good Ser! That is no way to address the son of a lord. Ser Bubbles here seeks an audience with our grand lord," booms the scout.

Bubbles appears lost in a trance. "My father…" He snaps out of it. "Yes. I must speak with your lord about my own. Tragedy has struck."

The guard sighs, fed up with foreigners, "And the girl?"

"She is my prisoner but speaks a tongue I do not understand. I have it on good authority that your grand healer may help."

"Very well. Right this way," the guard concedes.

Bubbles looks up at the scout. "Thank you, friend. What, might I ask, is your name?"

"I am Little Lord Cavalier of Bon Chevalier, son of Grand Lord Vigneron, though it seems the guards don't recognise me in my scouting armour. That one will see a week in the stocks for his rough tongue," he grins righteously.

Bubbles nods approvingly, then grabs his horse and prisoner, following the guard into the castle.

* * *

The rogue gates of Castle Bon Chevalier spring open with a creak, a cough, and a bah, as the snobby guard leads Bubbles and his prisoner into the courtyard. Inside the granite castle walls, Bubbles sees more market stalls, mostly smoke and wine sellers, along with luxurious cushions and blankets made of exotic materials strewn across the floor—people lay asleep everywhere, naked. *Bon Chevalier.*

The guard dismounts his snail and leads it to a damp, shaded corner where he ties its reins and gently pats its shell. His snail sucks its huge slimy head into its shell with a moist *pop*, setting itself to rest. The guard motions for Bubbles to tie Pearwood in the stables alongside his snail; Bubbles does so, noticing that every inch of this stable is covered with a thin layer of sticky slime. Pearwood licks at it, making Bubbles retch.

Bubbles is led inside the castle keep with the girl's fetters in hand. He noticed lavish portraits of snails holding weapons and conquering different parts of The Land of Linear.

As Bubbles and the guard approach the throne room doors to seek an audience with the grand lord, the guard barks at two fellow soldiers who had fallen asleep on duty, supposedly guarding the doors. *Bon Chevalier.*

Before entering, the guard turns to Bubbles, "A word of advice, foreigner, the grand lord likes to be referred to as Papa Escargot. And you should greet him in our native tongue of Franglaise. *Bonj-ello.*"

"Bonj-ello," Bubbles says in practice.

The guard pushes the throne room doors open, and Bubbles and his prisoner enter.

As he walks down the grand red carpet leading up to the throne, Bubbles looks around in astonishment. *What a lavish place,* he thinks to himself. Red grapes hang from the ceiling lit up by some type of lightning-harnessing light source, gold specs line the granite walls and floor, and a red wine fountain in the shape of an angel pissing embellishes the centre of the room. He walks around the fountain, smelling the acidic notes of sweet summer wine fill the air.

With his stupefied eyes—not his ears—he spots the Grand Lord of Bon Chevalier sitting atop his pure gold throne, shaped oddly like a commode.

As he looks up at the grand lord, Bubbles is surprised to find a few things. Firstly, his nakedness. It's his land, his castle, but surely the gold throne is cold on his arse. Secondly, the two giant golden-shelled snails that sit at his feet. And thirdly, that the two giant snails not only sit at the grand lord's feet but suckle on his toes, making him giggle.

Giggle, giggle.

This sight takes Bubbles aback, causing him to stumble on his words as he says, "Bonj—" he pauses, finger to lip, thinking.

"Speak, foreigner!" the grand lord demands. "In fact, why don't you start by explaining why your helmet remains on your head in my court? It is disrespectful to address a grand lord in such a manner."

Bubbles spots Little Lord Cavalier standing by the grand lord's side. He nods at Bubbles. At the same time, the guard that greeted them outside the castle realises to whom he spoke so harshly and gulps whilst pulling at his collar.

"Bonj—Bonj-ello, Papa Escargot. My apologies. Since my journey along the desert roads, my helmet has been stuck. No amount of pulling or pushing will make it budge," Bubbles explains with a bow.

The grand lord relaxes into his chair and retches at Bubbles, as if to say he's already lost interest in his plight.

Giggle, giggle.

"What business have you in my castle?" the grand lord asks.

"I bring grave news from the Bastion of Beer. My father, the Grand Lord of Beer, is dead," Bubbles says, looking at the floor. The court gasps. He continues, "We believe this girl is responsible. She was found covered in his blood in his bedchambers."

"Your father? You must be his son," the grand lord surmises, obviously.

"Yes. His youngest, Ser Bubbles of Beer."

"I'm sorry for your loss, boy. Your father and I fought side-by-side in many battles."

"He always spoke highly of you, Papa Escargot. But that's not all. You know of our legendary Holy Stein O' Kin?"

"I've heard whispers." The grand lord pinches his eyes together.

"It's been stolen, and two ogres appeared shortly after." The court takes a collective breath.

"Ogres! They are a thing of legend—a folktale, a farce." The grand lord hesitates in disbelief. "And what of the girl? Why have you brought her here?" he inquires.

Bubbles pushes the girl forward. "Speak," he says. They watch her intently. "Speak!"

"*Bethison,*" she hisses.

Giggle, giggle.

The grand lord strokes his chin. "Hm. An ancient language, I believe, similar to our own." He turns to Little Lord Cavalier. "Fetch Grand Healer Peu-de-Polis, *Few Hairs* to you foreigners. He is trained in these matters."

Whilst his son exits the room, the grand lord sniffs awkwardly as the discourse grinds to a halt. "So, Ser Bubbles…"

Giggle, giggle.

"Lovely weather out there, isn't it?" He says, grasping at straws.

"Indeed, Papa Escargot. Your land is beautiful." Bubbles smiles.

"Um…" The grand lord taps his fingers on his throne's arm.

Tap. Tap. Tap.

The uncomfortable silence echoes through the room.

"Ah…The fountain behind you, Ser Bubbles. Have you seen anything like it before?" he asks, grasping at more straws.

"Never. I noticed the luxury of this castle the moment I stepped inside."

"Well, that's nice to hear," he giggles.

The grand lord hums to himself. *Bum de bum, de bum.* "Sorry about your father. How are your brother and sister coping?"

"They are strong, Papa Escargot. My brother will make a fine ruler," Bubbles says, cutting the atmosphere.

"That he will…" *Bum de bum.*

Giggle, giggle.

The doors creak open and Little Lord Cavalier enters with the Grand Healer of Bon Chevalier, relieving the awkward small talk.

"Papa Escargot." Grand Healer Few Hairs bows, showing his tonsure. "I hear of an ancient tongue being spoken in our court."

"Yes, Healer. This—" He gestures toward Bubbles. "—is Ser Bubbles of Beer. His father has been murdered by this girl, and the Holy Stein O' Kin is missing."

"Lords above!" Few Hairs expresses. "A tragedy, Ser. A tragedy indeed."

The grand lord continues, "And this girl speaks a language we don't understand."

"I believe she can offer us some answers," Bubbles interjects. "Speak, girl." He prods her.

She growls, "Bethison."

"Bethison…" Few Hairs ponders her tongue, hand to mouth, his brown robes slouching down his arms. "Anglanch, my lords—The ancient language of sorcerers. Today it is spoken by few, but remains the preferred tongue of the *Cup 'n' Sorcerers.*"

"Well…What is it that she says?" Bubbles asks, growing impatient.

"Bethison…" He pauses. *"Betrayal."*

Bubbles tilts his head like a confused puppy, "Betrayal?"

"Let me ask you this:" the grand lord speaks up. "Who's serving girl is she?"

"My sister's, Little Lady Alesing," Bubbles says, innocently.

"Perhaps, your little lady sister wishes to be more grand," Papa Escargot suggests.

CHAPTER 9

Little Lady Alesing delicately runs her fingers along the bumpy, melded glasses, mugs, and steins of Beer's throne—*The Plastered Throne*, a detail likely lost to your memory through the previous chapters. She is alone as she regards the seat ambitiously.

The dust settles around her, and with one timid step, she moves toward the throne. She takes a deep breath, inflating herself with confidence. Finally, as she teases the throne's arms, Alesing turns and takes a seat. A malevolent look appears on her face. *The people of Beer will bow before me, the first Grand Lady of The Land of Linear,* she thinks to herself.

With an incensed crash, the throne room doors fly open and Ser Hops storms up to Alesing, his face like thunder.

"So it's true then, sister?" asks Hops.

"What is that, Brother?" Alesing asks, playing innocent despite herself.

"There have been whispers amongst the village folk that a woman looking much like yourself is turning people into ogres." A vein on Hops' forehead begins to pulsate, his palms grow sweaty, his knees weak…He feels like an Eminem song.

"Ogres, Brother?" she laughs. "That requires magic. Have you ever known me to use magic?"

"No, sister. But you are sitting on the throne when it is not your place to do so—"

"I am the eldest child of the late Grand Lord Slosh of Beer!" she roars. "It is my rite."

"That is not the law of the land, sister. Father wished for I to sit upon the throne. It is you who denies my rite," Hops explains, puffing up his chest.

"Well, dear Brother, I am changing the law of the land."

"You've always wanted this, haven't you?" Hops snarls.

"Not at all. Only, since father's death, I do not believe you are fit to rule these lands," she says, prodding Hops' fragile ego.

"It's true that I have not always been strong enough, but—" Something inside Hops clicks. "Father's death." He chuckles with disbelief. "It was your serving girl, was it? Of course. And The Stein, I suppose that was her, too."

"What are you trying to suggest, dear Brother?"

"That I'm a god damned fool, Sister." His eyes well up as he turns to leave the room.

"Where are you going?"

"To join my brother in Bon Chevalier. To tell him that not only is our sister a usurper, but a—" his voice breaks, "—murderer too! And a thief. Goodbye, Alesing."

"Brother, you've not even the tenacity to challenge me. This is why you cannot sit upon the throne."

"And you've not even the sense to deny my accusations," he cries, moving toward the door.

"Beasts!" Alesing shouts. "I'm sorry, Ser Hops, but I cannot allow you to leave the castle."

Two ogres appear from behind the throne as if magically manifested into existence. Ser Hops looks at the beasts and falls to his knees, his eyes wide and mouth agape.

"Swear fealty to me, Brother. Accept my rule, and I will let you live. Deny me and become one of them," Alesing commands.

The wretched ogres move aside Hops, gripping their mammoth hands around his tiny arms. They pull him to his feet. His body gives up and hangs in their grip like a deflated balloon.

"A murderer. Patricide, no less. You expect me to be your loyal servant?" he spits.

"Perhaps this will change your mind." She snaps her fingers. "Beast, bring me a villager."

One of the ogres holding Hops lets go and leaves the room whilst the other tightens his hold on Hops' arm. The ogre returns with a beaten and battered man—the village baker. He is presented on his knees beneath the throne.

Alesing slowly steps down, standing in front of the baker. She gently tilts his head up by his chin, smiling comfortingly. "Thank you, citizen."

"The Stein!" she commands, and an ogre stomps off to fetch the legendary vessel.

Hops realises what's about to happen. "No! Sister, no! He is an innocent man."

"He wants my mercy." She turns to the baker. "Don't you want my mercy?" The man shakily bows his head as the ogre returns and hands Alesing The Stein filled with beer of Beer.

Alesing touches the baker's head. "Here, drink this." He scrambles to sip from The Stein as she tilts it upwards and speaks words incomprehensible to Hops, similar to her serving girl. Her eyes roll back into her head as she chants a demonic prayer, and her hair flies up, levitating.

"Sister…" Hops whispers.

"Become ma bete…Become ma bete…Become ma bete," Alesing chants.

With a flash of white light between the baker's head and her hand, Alesing is pushed back by force, and the baker's body flops to the floor, lifeless.

"No!" Hops protests as he struggles against the ogres grip.

The baker starts coughing, his body spasming and writhing with pain. Hops' jaw hangs low whilst he watches. The baker's muscles tear through his skin, turning green as they react with the air. First, his arms bulge through, then his legs, then his torso, and finally, yellow fangs sprout from the bottom of his jaw as his face turns a sickly colour. Blood spatters from the baker's mouth. He sits up with a horrifying roar.

"Arise, my dear beast," Alesing commands. The new ogre does as she bids, stoutly planting his feet beside her.

"So, you *are* a sorceress, sister," Hops confirms.

Alesing smirks. "That is your fate, Brother. Unless you swear fealty to me."

Hops shakes his head, sighing. "I loved you, you know? I always thought that you were so smart and brave. And I always knew you'd make a brilliant ruler."

For a second, a flicker of humanity flashes before Alesing's eyes as Hops continues, "This, sister. This isn't ruling. This isn't you. This is evil. And I am sorry for whatever forces have poisoned your mind."

Alesing regards Hops with contempt and sorrow, surprised by her own emotions. She sniffles to her beasts, "Take him…" She inhales her feelings. "Take him to the dungeons."

CHAPTER 10

As the sorceresses word for betrayal echoes through the throne room of Bon Chevalier, the grand lord, Papa Escargot, leans forward.

Giggle, giggle.

"Cup 'n' Sorcerers, you say, Grand Healer Peu-de-Polis?" he asks, seemingly intrigued.

"Yes, my lord," Few Hairs confirms.

"How certain are you? They are a powerful sect."

"Their tongue is the exact opposite of ours. Where we speak Franglais, they speak Anglanch. I am certain." He nods.

Giggle, giggle.

Papa Escargot strokes one of his giant snails, tutting, "This will not do. Their order has not interfered with kingdom life for centuries. Why now?"

"An opportunity, perhaps. If what we fear is true, they may see this as their chance to build an army and rule the lands under their dark forces," Few Hairs suggests.

"An army?" Bubbles asks quizzically.

"If they have chosen your sister as their means to rule, Ser Bubbles, she is likely a sorcerer too. She will have no trouble commanding The Bastion of Beer against you," the healer explains.

"Then, I must go at once. And stop my dear sister and secure The Stein and save the people of Beer from her dark magic," Bubbles says, not a semblance of hesitation. *And remove this tiresome helmet so I can enjoy a cold pint*, he adds in his head.

"Are you mad, boy? You are but one man," giggles the Grand Lord of Bon Chevalier as his snails work their way up his ankles.

Bubbles falls to his knees, bowing his head. "Papa Escargot, you are correct. I am but one man. If what your healer says is true, my sister is strong. I ask, humbly, for your help. Please, allow me to command your army," he says solemnly.

The Grand Lord of Bon Chevalier rolls his eyes and leans back in his throne. "Rise, boy. I will not commit an army to your cause."

"Father! The Beerians are our allies," Little Lord Cavalier gasps.

Giggle, giggle.

"Quiet, son." He dismissively waves his hand. "I will not give you an army, Ser Bubbles. I simply do not believe the legend of your Stein. Ogres! What you saw was likely an elaborate trick by the sorcerers to weaken your will. I am sorry, Ser Bubbles. However, I will imprison the girl and deal with the Cup 'n' Sorcerers myself. They must not be allowed to continue unchecked."

"With all due respect, Papa Escargot, ogres *are* real. Right now, there are two imprisoned in The Bastion of Beer dungeons. I implore you—" Bubbles begins to beg.

"Be that as it may," booms the grand lord. "I cannot ask my men to die for a cause that may very well exist only in legend." He pauses to regard Bubbles' conviction. "I knew your father well, boy. So—" He turns to Few Hair's. "—send word to the Cup 'n' Sorcerers that we have one of their own. And tell them that if they do not cease their dark doings in Beer, they will face the legendary army of Bon Chevalier in battle. Guards." He claps. "Take the girl to the dungeons."

Two guards surround the serving girl; one holds her rope, the other follows behind. She whispers demonically as she's removed from the throne room.

"My lord, Papa Escargot, you honour me, and my late father," Bubbles says earnestly.

"That I do, Ser Bubbles, but you will see that it does not come to war," he commands. "The threat of my army should be enough to deter these witches."

"I will do my damndest, Papa Escargot," Bubbles promises.

"You will do better than that," the grand lord grunts. "Take two of my men to escort you safely back to Beer."

"Father!" Little Lord Cavalier interjects. "Let me travel with Ser Bubbles. I believe I can be of great service."

A FANTASY NOVEL THAT GETS STRAIGHT TO THE POINT

The Grand Lord of Bon Chevalier sighs, "You see, Ser Bubbles, the trouble you are already causing? One whiff of adventure and the boy's chomping at the bit like a whore after coin. No, son, you will stay here. This isn't your story—your presence in Beer complicates the upcoming plot too much. Why you were written in to be my son in the first place, I don't know."

Little Lord Cavalier steps back in disappointment, rolling his eyes and sighing like a jilted teenager. "Yes, Father. The plot is important, I suppose," he submits.

"Now go, Ser Bubbles. Do what you can to save Beer." The grand lord dramatically points forward toward the door.

"Yes, Papa Escargot. Thank you for lending me your men."

And so, after retrieving his horse, Pearwood, from the damp stables, Bubbles sets upon the road back to The Bastion of Beer, hoping not to encounter any Jive Turkeys this time. As he makes haste, the two Bon Chevalierian soldiers trail behind him on their snails. Honestly, they're not much help due to their terribly slow speed and serve only to create two sticky lines of slime along the road.

CHAPTER 11

Looking upon the pure white outer walls of Bon Chevalier castle, you couldn't imagine anything other than perfection, harmony, and wealth. Of course, as we know from the giant snails that nurse Papa Escargot's toes, that is not the case.

Yet, even more contrary to Bon Chevalier castle's outer appearance is its dungeons beneath—a menacing corridor of dark holes lit only by the imperceptible glare of candles from the light upstairs. The walls of the dungeon are wet and seething with mini beasts, dungeon snails—like garden snails but with a penchant for torture—and little-legged beetles. It's an all-around nasty place that keeps the local crime rate low. One poor soul who sits in a cell of this dungeon is the serving girl.

She sits curled into a ball in the corner of her cell, repeatedly hissing *bethion* to herself as if stuck in a loop. She rocks back and forth on the cold hard floor made soft by the springy exoskeletons of insects. *Bethion.* Is her head hollow, ravaged by magic? Only a sorcerer could know what happens beyond her wildly white eyes.

* * *

Storm clouds follow a lonesome hooded woman as she approaches Bon Chevalier castle. The door guards stand to attention crossing their battle axes. "Who goes there?" one guard dutifully asks. The woman offers no response. Instead, she stares at the ground, the only feature of her face visible, an elongated green nose adorned with warts. She takes a step forward, the clouds follow.

"I said, who goes there?" the guard demands.

The woman raises a hand and points a long arthritic finger at the guard's face. He moves his head back, confused.

"Seize—" the guard begins. "*Stocul*," the woman murmurs. Suddenly, he is enraptured by a flash of grey light. He stands, his body turned to stone, solid like a man in a strip club, unable to move. Dust crumbles from his sides—part of him is blown away by the wind.

The woman cranes her finger into the face of the remaining guard, whose knees knock together and teeth chatter. She opens her mouth to say the spell. "Sto—"

"Okay, okay. You want an audience with the grand lord, foreigner? Right this way." The remaining guard surrenders with a yawn; such is the resilience of a Chevilarian soldier. He takes her through the castle doors, along the courtyard wherein flowers and thickets wither upon her passing, and into the throne room. The ordinarily white walls grow grey with the shadow this woman brings. The guard presents the woman to the Grand Lord of Bon Chevalier. (You might be thinking, *what a coincidence that Papa Escargot is sitting in the throne room at precisely the right time.* It is a strange coincidence, isn't it? What are the odds?) Little Lord

Cavalier stands beside him whilst Grand Healer Few Hairs waits suspiciously by the door, listening intently.

Giggle, giggle.

"Guard, who is this woman you bring before me?" Papa Escargot demands with an air of outrage.

"I am unsure, Papa Escargot." He kneels. "She approached the gates and turned my fellow guardsman into stone," he whimpers.

"To stone?" Papa Escargot pauses in realisation. "So, sorcerer, you received word that we have one of your own."

The woman slowly lowers her hood, revealing her spotted green skin. She tilts her head with an uncomfortable creak, and, for a moment, Papa Escargot is certain he sees a centipede crawl across the whites of her eyes.

"Speak, witch!" the grand lord bellows.

"Brene la," she mutters, rough as gravel.

"Bring her, she says," shouts Few Hairs from across the room.

Giggle, giggle.

"Son." He turns to Little Lord Cavalier. "Fetch the girl."

"Yes, Father," Little Lord Cavalier responds, lightly jogging out of the room.

Probably best not to make small talk with this one, the grand lord thinks to himself with a finger resting on his lip.

Down below in the dungeons, dark as you like—or as described earlier—Little Lord Cavalier has the dungeon master unlock the girl's cell. The bright orange torch he holds lightens her cell. With a buzz, click, and rattle, the girl's bed of insects disperse, swarming into hidden cracks and crevasses. Cavalier pulls the girl to her feet. She howls at the fire in his hand. He drags her away with ease, for her body is merely a broken shell, out of the cell and up the stairs.

Meanwhile, Papa Escargot sits with a scowl on his face and a twitching nose as he and the green sorceress stare furiously at one another. Breaking the tension—kind of—Little Lord Cavalier returns with the girl. He throws her in front of the witch.

"Here," the grand lord says. "She has allegedly committed grave crimes against the people of Beer. What say you?"

From the floor, the serving girl looks up at the witch. The green sorceress, whose name is Power, whispers into the girl's head.

You are not a member of our order girl, she says.

I am a serving girl. I serve Little Lady Alesing of Beer, the girl replies.

She has trapped you in a powerful spell, the witch explains.

My body does not do as I ask, only what my lady commands.

Poor girl. I can grant you freedom from our sister's spell, the sorceress offers.

You would help me?

You are of no further use to our order.

Then please, release me, the girl begs.

It will come at a price, Power admits.

A price?

You must not be able to speak of what you have witnessed, the witch explains.

I promise. I will not whisper a word, the girl claims.

Very well.

Power begins chanting, *ripache sa langue, ripache sa langue ripach—*

"What is the meaning of this, Witch?" the grand lord demands, smashing his clenched fists on the arms of his throne.

Few Hairs takes a second to catch up, translating her words. "Rip out…" His eyes grow large. "Rip out her tongue, Papa Escargot. She says, *rip out her tongue.*"

Ripache sa langue.

Little Lord Cavalier steps forward to stop the sorceress's chant, but it is too late. The girl cries out as if being crushed by a castle wall. Blood spills from her mouth like paint, dripping down her body. She coughs and sputters, and with one grotesque wretch, she spits out her tongue. It lands at the feet of the grand lord, who recoils in disgust and covers his mouth to stop from throwing up.

The grand healer runs over to the scene, flushing pale at the emetic sight. He holds the girl's head up as her blood-spattered body lies limp on the floor.

"She's alive," he says, panting. "But not for much longer."

"Witch! I will give you one opportunity to release whatever hold you have over Beer and return *The Holy Stein O' Kin Beer* to its rightful owner," Papa Escargot seethes.

Power cackles, "The Stein is already in the hands of its rightful owner."

The grand healer drags the girl out of the centre of the room, sensing the coming confrontation. At the side of the room, he looks into the girl's eyes, watching her life fade away. She mouths, "Alesing. It was all Little Lady Alesing." Her eyes roll back, just as when she was under Alesing's spell.

"Guards, seize this sorceress!" the grand lord commands.

Little Lord Cavalier steps forward, drawing his sword. Several guards surround her. The sorceress raises her hood, maniacally laughing as she does so. She lifts her hands and points a finger at Cavalier and another at Papa

Escargot. At this, Little Lord Cavalier rushes forward, swinging his sword back.

From Few Hair's position, he sees a sweeping dust of grey light that covers the grand lord, his son, and the surrounding guards. *"No,"* he whispers as he quietly scampers to the throne room door. Before he flees the room, he looks on through the doorway. A once great grand lord, his heir, and personal guard transformed into a terracotta army.

Though, if Few Hair's was closer to the centre of the action, he would see that the grand lord has not been, in fact, turned into stone, but transformed into a tiny garden snail, quickly lapped up by one of his pets.

Gobble, gobble.

With haste, the Grand Healer of Bon Chevalier evacuates the keep, mounts a snail in the courtyard, and flies—as fast as a snail can fly—out of the castle gates, following Bubbles' guards' snail trails.

CHAPTER 12

All appears quiet on the horizon as Ser Bubbles of Beer and his two Bon Chevalierian guards approach The Bastion of Beer. The gulls squark, the sun sizzles, and the barley fields sway with a shimmer in the wind.

As they close in on the outer village, ambling through its roads, Bubbles' eyes squint suspiciously as he notices something peculiar. The babble of the morning markets, the laughing of street urchins pickpocketing tourists, the steam of fried food, and the splashing of ale are nowhere to be heard. All that Bubbles hears is the flapping of a wooden door bashing against the side of a hut.

Bang. Bang. Bang.

It pierces the silence.

"Ok, men. Let's dismount," Bubbles orders, tying his horse to a hitching post outside the local tavern. "This place is a ghost town. It's usually bustling with life and screaming with drunks." Bubbles chuckles sentimentally. "Usually one of those drunks in my father," he sighs. "Noble guardsmen of Bon Chevalier, I appreciate your assistance getting me here safely. Now, please, help me search the village for signs of life."

"Yes, Ser," the guards say in trained unison.

"I suggest you start with Layman's Library on the other side. It's used as a point of refuge in times of crisis."

The guardsmen turn and march off toward the other side of the village, investigating crevasses and hiding spots as they go. Meanwhile, Bubbles' eyes are drawn to the adjacent tavern like a moth to a flame, a quantity surveyor to a quantity, a drunk to a beer.

Well, I might as well search in here, might find something important, he convinces himself.

Usually a hub for exceptional village craic, Bubbles enters to a tavern of empty seats and closed shutters. Though, the beer taps are still in working order.

He walks behind the bar, passing a smoking candle only recently snuffed out.

Bubbles considers the candle, but shrugs it off with thoughts of beer.

From behind the bar, Bubbles grabs a stein and puts it under a tap protruding from the wall, labelled *Beer's Best*. With his back turned away from the door, he happily hums to himself, lost in his own world. The stein is full. He turns off the tap.

Right, now…how do I?… he uncomfortably fiddles with the rim of his helmet, trying to fit the stein through the small gap. *Come on…This helmet…Oh, bloody hell.* Try as he might, sipping a cold beer is an impossible feat, perhaps more unlikely than defeating the Cup 'n' Sorcerers. So, he sets on a new strategy, jilting his arm and splashing beer into his face attempting to catch it with his tongue like a cat playing with the rain—or, more accurately, like the idiot son of the late Grand Lord of Beer.

So focused on drinking his beer, Bubbles fails to notice the low rumbling noise behind him.

Maybe if I... he pokes his tongue out of the slit in his helmet, his armour dripping with nectar. *Ah, ha!*

A shadow covers the bar—a particularly grumpy shadow. Bubbles slowly turns, his tongue stuck in his beer. *Oh...*

Bubbles frantically launches his stein at the beastly ogre in front of him as it stretches its goliath mouth and roars wildly, spewing phlegm across the bar. Bubbles stumbles backwards, his back against the wall as the monster approaches the bar. Instinctively, Bubbles reaches for his scabbard, unsheathes his sword and shakily points it at the beast.

"Stay back, ogre or I'll cut you down like a sickly tree!" he warns.

The ogre doesn't listen. In fact, it does the opposite of listening, partly because ogres have terrible hearing from all the beeswax in their ears, but also due to the comparatively tiny size of Bubbles. The beast lurches forward into the bar, and at that very moment, Bubbles pushes his blade mightily through the ogre's chest. It pauses and staggers backwards with a confused whine.

"That's right, beast!" Bubbles sighs with misplaced relief. "Wait a minute..." He recalls the two ogres he and Ser Hops faced in the castle. Their weapons had been of no use. "Oh balls..."

The ogre looks at its chest, regarding the sword piercing its body. It wraps its vast ogre hands around the sword and pulls it out as easily as it would remove a toothpick from pineapple and cheese. The beast howls as it stomps towards Bubbles, who cowers behind the bar.

This is it, I guess, Bubbles submits.

As the ogre leans forward to wrap its huge hands around Bubbles' head to pop him like a ripe tomato, its eyes disappear in a spatter of yellow blood. Between its brow sticks a blackened blade. It chokes and falls backwards, spraying brains across the floor. Bubbles looks up, mouth agape and eyebrows raised. *What happened?*

"So Papa Escargot was wrong. Ogres do indeed exist," a voice says from across the tavern in a wise Franglais accent.

Bubbles pulls himself up, leaning on the bar as he does so. "Grand Healer Few Hairs," Bubbles gasps.

"Only a black blade can kill a black soul, Ser Bubbles," he cooly explains.

"What are you doing here?" Bubbles asks as he wipes ogre innards from his armour.

"Shortly after your departure, a sorceress arrived for the girl. She turned the entire court to stone. I was lucky to escape with my life."

"That's terrible," he pauses,
"He had it coming to him the moment he refused to believe you," Few Hairs admits.

"But you *did* believe me?"
"From the moment you entered the court."

"How did you get here so fast?" Bubbles wonders curiously. "It's a few days from Bon Chevalier."

"I rode the slime of your guards' snails. Their tracks created a slipstream of sorts," he explains as if it's normal. "What is your plan, Ser Bubbles?"

"I'm not sure. The guards lent to me are searching the village for signs of life, but after encountering this ogre, I'm sure they won't find any." Bubbles looks away with a grave expression.

"Your sister is likely raising an army of ogres for the Cup 'n' Sorcerers using the missing civilians. There will be more of these beasts," Few Hairs determines.

"If that is true, then I cannot set out to kill the ogres. That would leave Beer barren and kill hundreds of innocent people." Bubbles slumps onto a stool, his chin resting on his knuckles.

"There is a school of sorcery that believes magic devices are bound to their user. The device lends the sorcerer its magic." Few Hairs rubs his chin thoughtfully.

"What does that mean, Healer?"

"Destroy the bond, destroy the magic," he explains, waving an authoritative finger. "Kill your sister or destroy The Stein."

"My sister?" Bubbles rests his head in his hands. "I cannot do that."

"You will somehow need to retrieve The Stein from The Bastion of Beer, then. A challenge, given the beasts that lie behind those walls."

"Perhaps we could break in—I know the castle well, after all—and steel The Stein from under Alesing's nose," Bubbles suggests.

"For that, you will need an expert thief. Sorcerers are not easily fooled." He winks.

"A thief?" Bubbles pauses. "We need a hobbit, you mean?"

"No, that would probably entail some kind of copyright infringement." Few Hairs shrugs. "A castle of this size, you'll likely need more than one thief, too."

"Where can I find a band of thieves?" Bubbles knocks on the table in ponderance.

CHAPTER 13

Twelve chapters ago, when you began this *utterly ridiculous journey*, you were greeted by the friendly question, *Fancy a pint?* And then introduced to Ser Bubbles of Beer sitting in a smoky tavern, struggling to drink his own due to his stubborn helmet. Now, we return to that tavern, known as *Here*, in which our story started. So, you could say, in a cruel twist of fate, that we've gone from there to *Here*. (If you recall, *There*—with a capital letter—is another tavern quite like this one, only with a much lower hygiene rating; *there*—without a capital letter—simply refers to a physical location. Confused? It doesn't matter anyway.)

When we left Bubbles, he had just asked the tavern maiden to introduce him to a table of free swords across the room.

"Actually, before you introduce me, mayhaps I could buy them a round of beer. Whet their appetites," Bubbles requests.

"For them blokes who're laughing at you?" The tavern maiden looks unsure. "Well...I suppose you are a knight of the realm. One of Beer, at that. You must be used to it."

With a knowing smile, Ser Bubbles says, "Yes, I'm trained to be both ferocious and polite." He realises her insult. "Wait. What do you mean I must be used to it?"

The tavern maiden ignores Bubbles and turns to walk away, but he gently grabs her by the arm. She sighs, "What now, Ser?"

"All right! You clearly haven't done your NVQ in customer service," he tsks. "Might I know their names?"

"Certainly. That one there, the one with the terribly unkempt beard and bald head, that's Brave Boros. Expert archer, I hear."

Bubbles nods approvingly, "Good to know."

"The one to his left, with the pompous demeanour, that's Lord Aaron of Cawk."

"A Lord free sword! What is the world coming to?" Ser Bubbles sighs. "Though I've never heard of Cawk."

"They make the bottle stoppers for Bon Chevalierian wine," she sniffs. "And that other one, the um—" she puts a finger to her lip in thought, fumbling in her west-country accent. "The um…The one whose…I'm not sure about the right term."

"Just say dwarf, woman!" Bubbles snaps.

"Yeah, well, the *dwarf* with the black eye and penchant for light print media such as *The Daily Raven*, The *Helios*, and *The Sunday Sun Dial*, that's Wimpy William."

"Wimpy William. A craven?" Ser Bubbles sighs once again.

"No, they call him that because he makes cowards of his enemies. He's also got a magic ass tied up in the stables."

"Hm. A magic ass, who'd have thunk it? Excellent." He places a silver coin in the maiden's hand. "For your troubles." Bubbles gets up with a slight wobble and ambles over to the free swords' table.

He may not have been able to enjoy a cold pint, but the acrid smoke emanating throughout the tavern is enough to make any man—woman, beast, sorcerer, ogre, footballer—feel tipsy.

"Gentlemen!" Ser Bubbles gleams, arms open, as he approaches the free swords' table.

The men nod, unabashed and arrogant.

"I appear to have found myself in quite a predicament."

"What might that be?" Brave Boros asks with a rough northern voice.

"Well, I'm sure you heard my conversation with the lovely tavern maiden." Ser Bubbles lowers his arms.

"We might 'ave." Boros' lips barely move as he speaks.

"I won't bore you with another twelve chapters of details, so in case you're not fully caught up, let me give you a summary. A few days ago, my father, brother, sister, and I were enjoying—"

"What do ye wan' from us?" Wimpy William growls with a thick Scottish accent (because aren't all fantasy dwarves Scottish?).

Ser Bubbles' face drops with an awkward chuckle.

"I think what my friend here is trying to say is, how might we be of assistance?" Lord Aaron of Cawk interjects with a soft posh voice, diffusing the tension.

"Right. To the point, I'll get." Bubbles eyes William, who raises the corner of his lip like a cornered hound. "I'm looking for a merry band of thieves to help break into The Bastion of Beer."

"Thieves we may be, merry we are not," declares Ser Boros.

"Excuse these two buffoons. They failed to have their porridge this morning, as you can tell," Lord Aaron apologises. "The Bastion of Beer, you say? That's a well-fortified castle, is it not?"

"As fortified as any, but I know it like the back of my hand," Bubbles explains.

"And who might you be?" Lord Aaron inquires.

"Ser Bubbles of Beer, son of the late Grand Lord Slosh of Beer," he announces with pride.

"A knight! Asking for our assistance. Surely you have an army of men at your disposal."

"I did, but my sister, Little Lady Alesing, has since commandeered the castle with the help of the Cup 'n' Sorcerers. She murdered my father and has stolen..." He pauses. "How much do you know of *The Holy Stein O' Kin Beer?*"

"We've heard whispers," Lord Aaron says.

"My sister has taken it for herself and raised an army of ghastly ogres with a mind to rule Beer."

"So you wan' us t' steel back t' Stein. Wass in it for us?" Brave Boros asks bluntly. "They might call us free swords, but free we are not."

"Yes, it's a tad misleading, really," Lord Aaron quips.

"You like beer, don't you?" Bubbles asks as the maiden arrives with their drinks.

They collectively nod in agreement, murmuring their approval.

"What if I promised you a lifetime of free beer? You can have any beer, ale, or mead you desire—for the rest of your lives. The Bastion of Beer has plenty."

The free swords consider this amongst themselves, taking too long for Bubbles' patience.

"And," he adds, "I'll pay whatever you owe the tavern maiden."

Lord Aaron looks at his companions, who shrug and pull upside-down smiles as people do when agreeing to a good deal. He says, "Sounds reasonable." He gets up from the table and grabs Bubbles' hand, shaking it. "Looks like you've got yourself a band of—" He looks at the others. "—not so merry thieves."

"Brilliant. Maiden!" Bubbles calls. "I'd like to pay these gentlemen's bar tab."

"That'll be eight golds and 120 silvers," she calls back.

Bubbles' face grows pale.

"What have you boys been drinking?" He pulls at his sweaty collar, or he would if he wasn't wearing armour. "To Beer, we ride."

And that they do. Bubbles on Pearwood, Lord Aaron on his black steed, Brave Boros on a standard issue nag, and Wimpy William floating beside them on his magic ass.

CHAPTER 14

"Snails!" Wimpy Williams huffs as Bubbles and his band of not-at-all-merry thieves arrive in Beer. They dismount and amble toward the village tavern.

"Yes, they belong to the Bon Chevalierians sent here to assist my endeavours," Bubbles explains.

"Ah, we shall get along famously. My family has provided their corking equipment for hundreds of years," Lord Aaron of Cawk boasts.

"Slimy bastards," grunts Brave Boros with a northern twang.

"Come on, play nice," Lord Aaron says.

"How can anyone ride one of those things? They give me the—" Wimpy William shudders. "—heebie-jeebies." He cautiously reaches a finger towards a snail hitched on a nearby post, but pulls back as it twitches its elongated black eyes. He shivers, then hitches his magic floating ass as far away from the snails as this side of the village will allow.

"Apparently," Bubbles starts, "if you ride on another snail's slime, they fly quicker than a—"

"Dwarf down a waterslide?" Lord Aaron quips, being met by laughter from Boros. William fumes, literal steam expelling from his ears with a high-pitched whistling noise like a train.

"You ought to be careful, Lord Aaron, else you'll find my axe embedded in yer kneecaps," William threatens.

"Oh, it's all in good fun, friend. I'll get you a beer as a token of my goodwill," Lord Aaron promises.

Wimpy William grunts his approval.

"Well, funny you should say that, Lord Aaron, because I suspect the grand healer is in this tavern," Bubbles says. The gang enter to find Grand Healer Few Hairs hunched over a table in the centre of the room and the two Bon Chavalierian guards standing at the door. Wimpy William and Brave Boros aggressively eye the guards, attempting to assert dominance—the guards' gazes are not broken.

"A guard of Bon Chevalier, are ye?" William asks one. "Looks more like a Clubland bouncer t' me," Boros says to the other. Lord Aaron approaches Few Hairs ahead of Bubbles whilst the others continue to berate the guards, who stare stoutly onwards.

"Ah, the Grand Healer of Bon Chevalier!" Lord Aaron welcomingly claps his hands together and sits opposite Few Hairs.

Few Hairs looks on, irritated by Lord Aaron's air of pomposity. "And who might you be?"

"Lord Aaron of Cawk. Free sword." He shakes Few Hair's hand against his will. "Pleasure. You know, my family has been Bon Chavalier's number four supplier of corks for hundre—" Lord Aaron is interrupted by a ruckus noise behind them.

Few Hairs turns to see the dwarf tightly grasped in a headlock and Brave Boros pinned to the wall with a sword to his neck whilst Ser Bubbles holds his head in his hands.

"Your expert thieves, Ser Bubbles?" Few Hairs asks sarcastically.

"They're a—" he searches for the right word, "—feisty bunch."

"Guards. Let them go," Few hairs commands. The Guards drop the two thieves and return to their positions by the door as if nothing ever happened.

William rubs his neck. "You're lucky you caught me before I could grab my axe."

"Aye, caught me at a funny angle, s'all," Boros says, protecting his ego.

"That's enough, gentlemen," Bubbles sighs. "Lord Aaron, kindly grab your companions a drink. Grand Healer Few Hairs, this is Wimpy William." He points to the dwarf who salutes with his axe. "This is Brave Boros." He belches. "And you've already met Lord Aaron of Cawk. This, as you've quite rightly guessed, is my band of thieves."

"And what a band we are!" Lord Aaron says with a cheeky smile as he slams three steins onto the table. "Boys, your drinks. The first of many, I'm sure."

Boros and William saunter over to the table, rub their sore parts and sit down. Bubbles stands at the far end of the table.

"A map of Beer castle, Healer?"

"Oui, the guards found it in the blacksmith's shop. It's notated with every entrance, exit, and weak spot," he explains.

"Looks like someone else had eyes on yer castle, Ser Bubbles," Wimpy William suggests.

"Indeed. We needn't use it anyway. I know beer like the back of my hand," Bubbles announces whilst holding the palm of his hand to his face. "Balls…"

"Do you have a plan, Ser Bubbles?" Few Hairs asks. Bubbles scratches his imaginary beard. "Well…The Bastion of Beer is a heavily fortified fortress—"

"Looks wonky t' me," interjects Boros.

"That's because each brick was laid by the drunken forefathers of Beer—the sloped walls symbolise their dedication to fermentation."

"To the point, Ser Bubbles." Few Hairs prompts.

"Ah, yes. There are three ways into the castle." He points to the door on the map. "Here, but walking in through the front door would be reckless. So, we can scale the front wall under cover of darkness."

"Won't there be guards patrolling the wall?" Lord Aaron asks.

"Most likely, but Brave Boros, I hear you're a crack shot with a bow and arrow."

"Aye, I never miss," Boros declares.

"So, you can take out sentries. When we reach the top, the watch towers will be bolted, which means scaling down into the courtyard."

"Won't that put us in view of any guardsmen? Even under cover of darkness, no doubt we'll be spotted under torchlight," ponders Lord Aaron.

"Quite right." Bubbles scratches his chin. "What if…What if one of us were able to unlock the towers?"

"But these are the only ways in, are they not?" Wimpy William says.

"Three ways in, mon petit dwarf. Ser Bubbles has only described two," Few Hairs reminds the group.

"The third entrance is round the back, here—" He points at the map. "The dungeons. There's a cell window that sits just above the ground. Only, I'd never have thought of it before, because no *man* could fit through the hole."

"That's not much help then, Bubbles," the dwarf huffs as the rest of the group stares at him.

Lord Aaron shows his pearly-white teeth. "William, he said *no man* could fit."

"What are ye talking about, ye pompous git?" The penny drops, Wimpy William stands up, appearing smaller than before, and slams his fists on the table. "My height—"

"Or lack thereof," quips Boros, whose grin is quickly wiped away by a blow from the dwarf's fist. You see, feelings and emotions, particularly anger, are tightly condensed the smaller you are, resulting in a terrifyingly fragile condition known as *little man syndrome*. He continues, "My height will not be exploited!"

"But it's the only way in without drawing too much attention to ourselves," Bubbles protests.

"All mah life, I've been exploited, teased, and chewed out because of me height," William starts with a quivering lip. "Never again will I be reduced to ney more than a dwarf ye can throw."

Lord Aaron rubs his companion's back. "It's ok, William. No one's trying to reduce you to a dwarf they can throw."

"Bubbles, are these men touched by magic?" asks Few Hairs.

"I don't believe so, Healer."

"Then why are they so incapable of reason?"

Wimpy William starts to sob just as Brave Boros lunges over the table, holding his sword to Few Hairs' neck. He says, "Ridiculous as it may seem, us toughened free swords have feelings too, Healer. You dare to mock us?"

"It…" Few Hairs gulps. "—is not a time for feelings. If Ser Bubbles cannot retrieve The Stein, it won't just be The

Bastion of Beer lost to ogres. The Cup 'n' Sorcerers are an ambitious bunch. They will plague The Land of Linear for all eternity if they are not stopped now."

Brave Boros grits his teeth and pulls his sword away as if restraining himself.

"The healer is right, William," Bubbles says. "This time, your height will not be mocked but used to defeat evil. You will go down in history as *The Mighty Dwarf Who…*

"*Grew*," Few Hairs suggests.

Wimpy William curls his lip, showing his teeth, "Why I oughta…" Then, a strange thing begins to happen: Wimpy William's gelatinous dwarf belly jiggles as he laughs. "*The Might Dwarf Who Grew.* And I suppose there'll be a few extra coins in mah pay packet, Ser Bubbles."

"You can suppose, I suppose." *I'll end up having to pawn my bloody helmet at this rate, if I can ever get it off*, Bubbles thinks to himself. *Harhar, get my helmet off.*

"So, Ser Bubbles, it appears you have a plan," Few Hairs says.

"Indeed." Bubbles looks to the side. "Now, as for you, Healer, I was thinking—"

Few Hairs stands up from the table. "I'm sorry, Ser Bubbles, I wish you the best of luck, but I must travel to the Cup 'n' Sorcerer's lair in the *Definitely Evil Forest*. My place is not here."

"What? What for?"

"My people are frozen in stone; I must seek a remedy. Besides, I might be able to stop them myself," Few Hairs says with all the arrogance of the French…Sorry…*With all the arrogance of the Franglais.*

"But…" Ser Bubbles starts. "I need your help, Healer. You supported my cause even when your grand lord did not." A flicker of vulnerability peaks through Bubbles' helmet.

"Because your cause is righteous. Now, everyone, place your weapons on the table."

"Mah axe?"

"My short sword?"

"My bow and arrows?"

The free swords hug their weapons tightly to their chest as if protecting their babies.

"Please. I'm not going to take them away. I'm going to help you."

"Go ahead," Bubbles prompts.

The band of emotionally unstable thieves reluctantly place their weapons on the table.

"You too, Bubbles," Few Hairs says. Bubbles does so.

"Stand back, gentlemen." The Grand Healer of Bon Chevalier holds his hands over the weapons, chanting, *"Acieel noick pour courts noick."* An icy blue light flashes over their weapons, casting shadows on the walls. The silhouette of the dwarf stands tall—William notices this, fixing his ego. Bubbles notices that his shadow is smaller than the rest. *Why?* he wonders, thinking of the challenges to come.

The silver of the weapons glow blue, and with a *puff* and a *zap* of wizardry, they flash, settling into colours of deep black and grey.

"There. I've enchanted your weapons so that they may kill ogres," Few Hairs explains.

The thieves, and Bubbles, take back their weapons and hold them up to the light, examining their new shimmer.

"Now, I must be off."

"Thank you, Few Hairs. I hope our paths cross again." Bubbles nods. Few Hairs nods back then exits the tavern with the two Bon Chevalierian guards.

"Right then, men. Now we wait for nightfall," Bubbles says whilst looking at his band of ragtag free swords. *Can this really be done?* he wonders.

CHAPTER 15

Viridescent trees lightly rustle in the wind, their leaves sparkling under the sun; mother birds chip soft lullabies, and docile animals canter across the luscious scenery. The thing about the *Definitely Evil Forest* in which Few Hairs finds himself, is that it looks quite ordinary. Yet once travellers look a little deeper, they realise that what glistens on trees is not healthy green leaves but snot from mutant caterpillars, and that all the happily playing wild animals are without eyes. Even the wind, when you press your ear to the sky, stops blowing gently and begins whispering horrifying messages with the buzzing interference of an answering machine.

Hi sweetheart, it's your mum. I hate you. Few Hairs hears this tickle into his ear but knows better. Firstly, his dear old mother is deeply proud of him—he knows that, she says it all time, emphasised by the thousand crosses she marks at the end of her letters.

Secondly, Few Hairs is no fool of the forest, and as he, his snail, and his two guards slither deeper in, the evil becomes more obvious. In fact, the forest is so definitely evil that the Mancunian band Oasis have been banned from performing here after suggesting it was only *Definitely Maybe* evil.

As Few Hairs approaches the centre of the forest where the Cup 'n' Sorcerers reside, the wind begins to howl, swirling leaves through the air and angrily shaking trees. The ground appears pockmarked by withered shrubs, and the sky is covered by a canopy of dying tree branches. Everything creaks in a cacophony of cracking chaos. Few Hairs furrows his brow at the sound whilst his guards press their hands against their helmets, attempting to block the maddening tones.

Up ahead, through the tangled thicket, Few Hairs spots an unkempt dirt road that leads to a dilapidated wooden hut.

"Men, single file behind me. Follow that road," the grand healer orders his guards. Why he doesn't speak his own language whilst there are no foreigners around is a mystery that even Few Hairs himself can't answer. All he knows is that he feels compelled to speak English, probably for the benefit of you, dear reader.

They reach the hut and dismount from their snails. "Hitch the snails up to that low-hanging branch over there," Few Hairs commands, and the guards do so as he considers the rotting hut. Its brown wood is damp all over, its roof collapsing in on itself, and its windows…well…there aren't any windows. The hut, despite belonging to the most powerful witches in *The Land of Linear*, is, frankly, a shithole.

Bang. Bang. Bang.

Few Hairs knocks on the door.

The door slowly swings open with a pitter-patter and clatter, revealing an unassuming hooded woman. "Yes?" she croaks.

"I'm the Grand Healer of Bon…" He remembers what happened. "I *was* the Grand Healer of Bon Chevalier. I demand an audience with the High Sorcerers."

The woman looks up at him, flashing her siren-red eyes. "Come."

Few Hairs gestures to his men to follow him. "No," the woman snaps. "You enter alone."

Few Hairs chews his lips and looks at his men. "You heard the woman. Wait here."

The guards nod and fall into their default position—standing at either side of the door. Few Hairs enters the hut. The door flaps shut behind him. Shortly after, tree roots shoot up from the ground and wind themselves around the Bon Chevalierian guards, creeping into their mouths and suffocating them.

Inside, there is nothing but rot. No furniture, no people, just an empty hut.

"Right this way," the woman says.

"But there's noth—" Few Hairs notices a mouse hole in the corner of the hut, the floorboards crumbling into the crawlspace below. "Down there?"

The sorcerer winks a red eye, raises an arthritic hand, and snaps her fingers. Few Hairs watches with terror as the woman shatters into a million tiny black spiders—the ones with bobbly knees and hair-thin legs. The spiders swarms Few Hairs' feet and ankles. With a flash of magic, he is transformed into a defenceless garden snail, just like the Grand Lord of Bon Chevalier. He falls through the air, only to be caught by a crawling bed of spiders that carry him into the mouse hole.

Slipping and sliding as if on a hairy water slide, Few Hairs is flushed through a claustrophobic tunnel by the stream of spiders. His elongated snail eyes flap and flutter, at one point getting stuck to his shell. And he screams and hollers with a high-pitched voice until…

Plonk.

He finds himself in the Cup 'n' Sorcerer's lair, neatly hidden beneath the floorboards. Around him, Few Hairs sees a red mud trail leading to a rope bridge.

"Come," a bobbly-kneed spider croaks as it shuffles past him onto the bridge. He slithers behind with a sweaty brow. He looks over the edge to find a busy chasm of beetles, maggots, spiders, and centipedes clicking and rattling their goose-pimple-inducing babble.

As Few Hairs looks closer, he notices that this isn't simply a slew of bugs buzzing from place to place; there are caves in the side of the cliff—homes. And street lanterns line the rock face, illuminating the floor next to what appears to be a market.

I wonder what they're selling, the healer ponders to himself. *Evil elixirs, robes, and wart cream, no doubt.*

What feels like a cold hand slaps into Few Hairs' shell, jilting him out of his gaze. Strangely to Few Hairs, he realises he's moving along the bridge without moving himself.

Oh dear...

He bends an eye round to his side and notices a thick lump of fluffy white string stuck to his shell, pulling him along.

"This way, snail, before I eat you for lunch," hisses the spider as she pulls him to the other side. Few Hairs' protruding eyes jitter with a frigid feeling.

The spider guides the healer along the rest of the red mud road to a darkened door made of blackened bones. He feels a million eyes stare at him as they enter—not from a million bugs, but from 125,000 eight-eyed spiders.

At the end of the room sits a behemoth tarantula with leg hairs long enough to comb and silver eyes like mirrors, sat on a throne made of dusty cobwebs and dead flies. *The High Sorceress.* Beneath the tarantula sits three smaller but equally skin-crawling arachnids. One pink, one green, and one purple. *Power, Greed, and Beetroot.*

CHAPTER 16

Night has fallen. All the stars in the universe hang over The Bastion of Beer as if watching Bubbles and his gang of thieves sneak along the castle's right side. They use the vast shadow of the wall cast by the glowing stars and moon to their advantage, hiding in the darkness. Bubbles looks to the long plane of barley to his side, clenching his fists with determination as the fields rustle in the cold night breeze.

Sister, I can't believe you'd betray us like this, he thinks. *Please don't be truly evil when I find you.*

"What's this here, chaps?" Lord Aaron asks as they reach a small mudded mound highlighting an indent in the ground.

"I can't see in t' dark," Boros grunts.

"Hold on, I think I've got a match," William says, patting his pockets.

"No! No matches. We don't want to draw any unnecessary attention to ourselves," Bubbles says, raising his hands. "There's only one cell with a window on this side of the castle."

"In that case, Wimpy William, care to lend us a hand?" Lord Aaron asks.

"Do I have to do everything around 'ere?" William smirks as he kneels beside the barred cell window. He raises his enchanted axe and begins whacking the bars.

Bang!

Clank!

Boom!

"One more blow, and it'll be done!" Lord Aaron announces.

That's what she said, Brave Boros chuckles to himself. *Or is it what he said?*

William curves his axe behind his shoulders, winding himself up like a rusty tabletop toy.

Swish.

Clonk.

Clatter.

Creak.

The bars give way and fall to the bottom of the cell, hitting the cold stone floor with a metallic clang.

As Wimpy William's chest heavily rises and falls with exhaustion, the rest of the gang stands staring at him with uncomfortable smiles. He looks around and notices. "What now?"

"What you're doing for Beer, William, it won't be forgotten," Bubbles says, rubbing the back of his helmet.

"Right," gasps Boros. "Down you go then, dwarf."

"The things I do for coin and beer," William complains.

"Imagine what you'd do for love," Lord Aaron quips.

"Not this!" William snarls as Bubbles suddenly invents a new type of food in his head: meatloaf.

Wimpy William pushes himself onto his stomach and squeezes himself through the window. He groans and cusses whilst the others try to hide their sniggers.

"Shite!" William shouts, muffled as a result of his head being inside the cell. "I need some 'elp 'ere, lads."

The gang look down to see a rather stumpy pair of legs and a gelatinous rear frantically flailing.

"Boros, you seem to have an angry disposition—" Bubbles starts.

"—Give him a kick," Lord Aaron finishes, and Brave Boros gallantly does as he's asks. With one great stomp, Boros pops Wimpy William's lower half through the window. He smashes to the ground with a chaotic clank.

"Ye bastards! I'll have yer head, Boros," Wimpy William angrily shouts from inside the cell.

"Good luck William," Bubbles calls down. "Remember, we appreciate you allowing us to exploit your small size."

"Be off with ya!" William growls back.

"Right then, men." Bubbles smacks his hands together. "Our turn."

A FANTASY NOVEL THAT GETS STRAIGHT TO THE POINT

* * *

Slumped on his arse, Wimpy Williams dusts himself off and surveys the cell. The darkness is deep, making everything but figures and outlines invisible.

The bastards. Just because I'm a dwarf. Speciesist arseholes, he mutters to himself.

"Hello, who's there?" a quivering voice asks from the corner of the cell.

Wimpy William jumps back, startled, raising his axe. "A prisoner. Keep back, else you'll find mah axe crushing yer skull," William warns.

"I mean no harm. Were you sent to break me free?" the voice wonders with a glimmer of hope. "I knew they hadn't got to Bubbles. I knew he'd come back for me."

"Bubbles? Who are ya, prisoner?" Wimpy William approaches the man, still curled up on the floor, to get a better look. Golden robes covered in dirt and dust lay draped from the man's shoulders.

"Me? Well, I'm Ser Hops of Beer, rightful heir to the throne," Hops explains innocently.

"So, you're Bubbles'—"

"His brother, yes," Hops confirms.

"Well, what're ye doing down here?"

"My sister imprisoned me after I refused to swear fealty to her. Who…Who are you? Why are you here, stranger? They'll kill you if they find you. Or worse—they'll turn you into an ogre," Hops warns.

"I'm a thief, hired by ye brother, here to help retrieve The Holy Stein O' Kin Beer." He pauses dramatically as if he is renowned across the lands. "They call me Wimpy William." Hops meets him with no recognition.

"So he's trying to stop Alesing," Hops chuckles. "Always has been a ballsy bugger, my brother."

"He certainly has his charm," William says sarcastically. "I wonder if ye might lend me a hand, Ser…"

"Ser Hops," he reminds William.

"Ser Hops. I'm tryin' a get to the watch tower on the right side of the castle. Do ye perhaps know the way?" William inquires.

Ser Hops clamours to his hands and knees and pushes himself up from the floor, towering over William. "I know this castle better than I know myself," Hops says, because a direct answer would be too easy.

"That's a yes, then?" William confirms.

"Indeed."

"Take this." He hands Hops an enchanted dagger, then walks to the cell door, examining the lock.

"A lock made by a Beerian locksmith is hard to crack. They're always so drunk when designing the locks that they become incomprehensibly complex," Ser Hops notes.

Wimpy William disregards this statement and pummels the lock with his axe. Sparks fly as greasy determination washes over William's face.

The lock cracks under William's might, and the cell door creaks open. "There. Incomprehensibly complex, my arse."

"I thought you said you were a thief? Shouldn't you be quieter?"

"Aye, but we all have our ways of buggery an' burglary," William grunts in his Scottish accent.

CHAPTER 17

Their backs pressed to the wall, Ser Bubbles, Brave Boros, and Lord Aaron edge along the front of the castle, keeping out of sight of the above sentries.

"What's your aim like in the dark, Boros?" Bubbles asks.

"Well, I nearly blinded t' missus once." He cracks a smile out the corner of his mouth. "She couldn't see or walk straight for a week."

"What?" Bubbles tsks.

"Northerners, aye?" Lord Aaron raises an eyebrow."

"Your aim, Boros…Can you take the sentries down from here?" Bubbles clarifies his meaning.

"Ay'…thought you were asking about me cock."

"Why, at a time like this, would I be asking you about your penis?" Ser Bubbles asks, frustrated. *I wonder if my other helmet is stuck,* he quietly thinks to himself.

Brave Boros shrugs. "To answer your question, I could shoot the 'air off a sailor's crack."

"What does that even mean?" Bubbles strains his fists.

"It means that mah aim is—"

"Just take down the bloody sentries, will you? If you don't want to get caught and very possibly die, that is," Bubbles snaps.

"All right, southern puff. Keep your wig on."

"How could I possibly be wearing a wig right now? My helmet is stuck." Bubbles' angry tone persists.

"I was jus' a saying. Caww, what's got your goat?" Boros says, forgetting himself…and the situation.

Bubbles turns to Boros, bringing his face uncomfortably close. "My sister is apparently an evil witch trying to raise an army of ogres. My father is dead, as could be my brother, who is the heir to Beer. Meanwhile, a revered and dangerously powerful artefact has fallen into the wrong hands. Yet, you want to stand here and tell me about your cock."

"Was jus' trying to lighten t' mood," Boros raises his hands in apology.

"Now, can you please take out those bloody sentries, *Brave* Boros?" Bubbles asks sternly.

Brave Boros holds Bubbles' gaze for a moment, as if deciding whether to take out the sentries or punch Bubbles in the gut. Under the circumstances, he feels the former is a more aggregable option.

As Boros swoops out from the shadows, he pulls out his bow and draws an arrow. It's as if he momentarily transforms from a brutish free sword to a dainty ballerina, delicately dancing a…whatever dance ballerinas dance. Seemingly in one cohesive movement, he fires two enchanted arrows into the darkness at the top of the wall.

He lowers his bow and looks at the others.

"Well?" Bubbles asks as nothing happens.

Boros taps his foot. "Wait a second," he sniffs.

Thud.

An ogre slumps in front of Bubbles.

Thud.

Another ogre hits the ground in front of Lord Aaron. "Oh. Nice work, old chap."

Boros arrogantly nods, failing to notice the crippled ogre crawling toward his leg.

"Boros?" Bubbles asks.

"Yes?"

"Great work, but you're not finished just yet."

"What do you mea—" A cold, sweaty hand grips his ankle with a quiet growl. Boros kicks his legs, but the beast holds on tight, showing its teeth.

"Any 'elp, lads?" Boros requests, almost unphased by the ogre.

Bubbles steps forward, draws his sword and pierces the ogre's head. "There."

The ogre's blood spits onto Boros' legs, but its hand remains clasped around his ankle. He shakes it off and removes his arrow, wiping away the blood and returning it to its quiver. Boros joins the others under cover of the wall.

"Lord Aaron." Bubbles nods.

"My turn now, aye?" He wobbles his head with hubris.

Lord Aaron removes a long rope with a metal claw attached to the end from his waist and steps away from the wall whilst spinning the rope.

Whoosh.

Whoosh.

Whoosh.

The rope swings through the air faster and faster. As it reaches its peak speed, Lord Aaron throws it toward the top of the wall. It pierces the air, yet as it nears the top, the metal claw only scrapes the stone.

"Damn…" Lord Aaron gasps. "Watch out, chaps."

Bubbles looks up and is met with a face full of metal and a ringing in his ears.

"Good job that 'elmet of yours is stuck. Woulda ripped your face to pieces, otherwise," Brave Boros observes.

"Yes…" Bubbles replies, dazed and concussed. "I suppose it's not all that bad. Try again, Lord Aaron."

Lord Aaron swings his rope around again, gaining more speed than the last time and…

Clank.

The rope wraps around the above parapet, and the metal claw grips onto the stone.

"Up we go," Lord Aaron says smugly.

Bubbles turns to the rope and vigorously tugs at it to check its stability.

"You first, Ser Bubbles," Lord Aaron says.

"Me?" Bubbles exclaims.

"This is your mission, old chap. Not scared, are we? The rope's fine."

"No, it's not…" Bubbles looks to the side. "It's what's on the other side of the wall."

"Don't worry, baba Bubbles, I'll take it up t' rear and keep you safe," Boros says, unawares.

"Won't be the first time you've taken it up the rear, aye, Boros?" Lord Aaron quips with that pompous smirk of his.

Bubbles considers for a moment whether it's worse to be pummelled by an obese ogre or to stand there and listen to Brave Boros moan and joke with Lord Aaron. He turns to the rope and starts climbing. Lord Aaron follows behind Bubbles and Brave Boros behind him.

"To the top, old chaps!" Lord Aaron declares, pointing his finger upwards and nearly losing his grip.

What have I gotten myself into with these free swords? Bubbles thinks to himself. *I just hope Wimpy William's a little more competent.*

* * *

The dwarf rolls along the floor, curled up in a ball, knocking into Ser Hops' legs after throwing his entire body weight at the tower door.

"Blasted door!" he shouts.

A clank and rustle echo up the tower stairs.

"Get back. I think someone's coming," Ser Hops observes, leaning flat against the wall at the top of the stairs. Wimpy William tries to mimic Ser Hops' position, but hiding his podgy dwarf belly proves difficult.

The low growl of an ogre carries up the stairway, along with the thud of its boots.

"What do we do, William?" Hops asks, dagger held in his shaking hands.

"It hasn't seen us yet," William whispers. "Get behind it when it reaches us. I'll take it head-on. We can't let it escape, else we'll be swarmed by beasts."

"I don't know if I can," Ser Hops moans. "What if it's someone I know? I mean...before they were transformed?"

"It'll be a whole lot worse if we're caught," Wimpy William warns.

Ser Hops looks down at his shoes in contemplation.

"All right, it's coming. Get ready," William says.

A wide stinking ogre lands on the hallway with its sword raised, ready to cut down trespassers.

Swoosh!

Ser Hops nimbly dodges the ogre's swipe and quickly sneaks behind. He jumps on the beast's back and tries to bring his dagger up to its neck. Only, to make matters difficult for Hops and William, the tower hallway is particularly small, definitely not built for brawls.

The ogre smashes from side to side and into the bolted tower door as it tries to throw Ser Hops from its back.

Wimpy William follows the beast as it spins around, attempting to get in front and lunge.

"Hold 'im steady, boy!" the dwarf shouts, his axe expertly spinning in hand.

Wimpy William comes around, in line with the ogre's belly and lunges forward without care for his own well-being.

* * *

Nearing the top of the wall, Bubbles is caught off guard by a sentry leaning over the ledge.

"Wh-oo go-e-s t-h-e-re?" it snarls nastily.

"Boros, I thought you got them all?" Bubbles shouts, startled, his grip loosening.

The beast at the top starts whacking its sword against the tangled rope.

Thwack.

It's at this moment that Bubbles' body decides to go numb. Not the kind of numbness where you can't move your arms or legs due to pins and needles, but the kind where the back of your knees starts to sweat after a particularly spicy curry.

"Bubbles!" Lord Aaron calls up.

No...I can't do this...We're going to die... Bubbles thinks in his Madras-like haze.

"Bubbles!" Lord Aaron shouts again, as one of Bubbles' hands slips from the rope, causing the rest of it to judder unstably.

Thwack.

At least I tried, I suppose. Maybe an army of ogres isn't such a bad thing. They'll certainly protect Beer.

"Bubbles, you imbecilic! Get a grip. Come on."

Thwack.

Why did Alesing have to turn evil? Bubbles asks himself. *Bloody typical. You're living your life, enjoying a beer, then BAM! You're thrown into a hero's journey.*

"It's almost through the rope!" Lord Aaron's words bounce off Bubbles' ears, avoiding his eardrums.

Hops. Ah, poor Hops. I could probably save him.

Thwack.

A FANTASY NOVEL THAT GETS STRAIGHT TO THE POINT

Beer. Beer. Beer. A cold beer from The Bastion of Beer. Bubbles licks his lips. *I suppose if I die, I'll never be able to taste beer again…or see my brother. Oh…*

Thwack.

Fine.

Bubbles' limp hand reaches back onto the rope and he pulls himself up with a mighty pull. He lunges forward five feet, falling into the ogre at the top of the wall. Bubbles draws his enchanted sword whilst sitting on top of the ogre. He pushes the blade through the beast's chest. It sputters as it quickly dies.

Lord Aaron and Brave Boros make it up, too.

"What the bloody 'ell 'appened? You coulda killed us!" Boros shouts, panting.

"Sorry about that. I had a…a moment." Bubbles friendlily pats Boros on the shoulder.

"Well, we made it, at least," Lord Aaron gasps.

They hear a frantic banging coming from the tower on the right side of the wall.

"I do hope that's William," Lord Aaron says.

With a crash, the door flies open, and Wimpy William, Ser Hops, and a cretinous ogre come tumbling out.

"A little help!" the dwarf shouts.

Brave Boros draws an arrow, aims at the ogre's head, and lets loose. The arrow pierces through the beast's brain. It stops moving.

"Nice shot, you northern prick," William walks over to Boros and shakes his hand.

Hops reels, considering how close the arrow is to his face.

"Hops…" Bubbles mouths.

"Bubbles…" Hops looks over to his brother with wide, moist eyes.

"I worried you were dead, Hops," Bubbles gushes.

"Alesing…She threatened to transform me into one of…" He looks down at the dead beast. "One of them. But she couldn't bring herself to do it."

"Then there must be some good in her still," Bubbles says hopefully.

"I'm not sure, Brother. She transformed the baker right before my eyes. She's…She's gone mad." He pauses. "What are we going to do?"

"According to the Grand Healer of Bon Chevalier, if we break The Stein, we break the spell. So, we've just got to get to The Stein. Hence my not-so-merry band of thieves." He gestures to Lord Arron, Brave Boros, and Wimpy William, all of whom quietly nod and sniff, seemingly disinterested.

"The castle is heavily guarded, Brother. It won't be easy," Hops warns.

"I've got a plan, Hops, don't you worry," Bubbles assures his brother. *Don't you worry, because I bloody well am,* he thinks to himself privately.

"Plan?" Lord Aaron inquires. "I was under the impression that you were just making it up as we go along."

"I'm guessing it's not a good plan, then," Boros speculates.

"It'll do," Bubbles says nervously.

CHAPTER 18

Few Hairs approaches the webbed throne, the bobbly kneed spider edging him along. "Your Highness," the spider loudly whispers. "The Grand Healer of Bon Chevalier seeks an audience with you."

One by one, the giant tarantula's eyes turn on Few Hairs with a mechanical clank. With a staggered breath and wheezy intonation, The High Sorceress speaks, "You should be cast to stone, Healer."

"Yes, well, unlike the soldiers of Bon Chevalier, I had the foresight to run when I saw one of yours," he says sarcastically.

"One of mine? You speak as if we sorcerers are separate from the likes of you, Healer," she coughs.

"You play with dark magic, your highness. Two of your three disciples are *literally* called Power and Greed." The green and pink spiders hiss. Few Hairs slithers backwards and continues, "Your order was created for evil, to antagonize the peace of the lands."

"We do as we must, Healer. Word crawled our way that your grand lord had agreed to help Beer," she says, stomping a leg forward.

"The affairs of Bon Chevalier are of no concern to the Cup 'n' Sorcerers," he protests.

"Papa Escargot could have turned the Beer boy away…"

"You forget yourself, sorceress," Few Hairs says stoutly despite his terrifying surroundings. "Bon Chevalier has a long history with your order. Last time my ancestors stood idly by, you ravaged The Land of Linear, plunging it into darkness. My grand lord would not do the same."

The huge tarantula cackles, bringing its face only a few inches away from Few Hairs' eyes, its fangs dripping with poison. "What is it you want, Healer? Why have you come?"

"Your sorceress turned my people and my grand lord to stone. I seek to cure them—to break the stone spell," he explains with a gulp.

"And we wish to sit the true ruler of Beer on the throne. Too long have we witches been denied our birth rites. Why would we help your people when they are so committed to destroying us?" Her eyes flicker.

"Because..." Few Hairs chews his lip. "Because I am in possession of knowledge that you'll want to hear. That is, if you want *Little* Lady Alesing to *hold* the throne."

The High Sorceress regards Few Hairs with curiosity, her fangs twitching. She makes a clicking sound at the back of her throat like a dying toad, and her army of money spiders swarm Few Hairs, suspending him from the ceiling of the throne room with their webs. His eyes clack together as he flies through the air.

"Do not play games with me, Healer," the tarantula bellows. "Speak your knowledge."

Few Hairs feels the weight of his body pull against his shell, ripping his flesh. He moans uncomfortably. "The second son of Beer," he pants. "As we speak, he and a band of hired thieves are breaking into The Bastion of Beer with a mind to smash The Holy Stein O' Kin Beer. You know what that means."

The High Sorceress recoils, considering this information. "Release him," she commands, and he drops with a squelching noise as his slime sticks to the ground.

She shows off her evil laugh, clearly practised daily in the bathroom mirror. Her minions join in, creating a maniacal choir of cackling spiders. "You fool," she says.

Few Hairs regards this scene, befuddled.

"The truth is, Healer, your people—" She gnashes her fangs. "—are dead. We never bothered to craft a counter-curse."

The snail's protruding eyes hang to the floor. "No…" he mutters, crestfallen.

"Power. Greed. Beetroot." The High Sorceress looks to her disciples. "Warn Grand Lady Alesing of her brother."

The three smaller tarantulas swiftly scurry off, whizzing past Few Hairs.

"So," she continues, "not only are you without your precious grand lord, Healer, you've just betrayed your only hope of stopping our order."

Few Hairs looks into the spider's eight eyes, squinting. "I will not let you get away with this, sorceress."

"What on earth could a puny garden snail like yourself do to us?" she growls, swinging towards him.

"You see, witch, I am no ordinary healer. I am the *Grand* Healer of Bon Chevalier." Few Hairs smirks as much as a snail can smirk, and his fleshy grey body begins to glow a technicolour hue, much like a camp theatre production.

Pop. Pop.

His elongated eyes shrink to their base, transforming into two walnut-sized eyeballs, and a nose pokes out in-between. A nail at the end of a pink fleshy stick erupts from the side of his shell: a finger! And a thumb!

The colony of spiders recoil in confusion.

Few Hairs explodes out of his shell, returning to his usual human form and bursting through the floorboards of the dilapidated hut, destroying the hidden world beneath. He lies unconscious on the remains of the hut as a colony of insects frantically flee the scene, their homes demolished by Few Hairs' anthropomorphic eruption.

As he lay with his eyes closed and mouth open, one hairy spider weakly crawls along Few Hairs' chest, its legs crushed in the chaos. This spider, being the all-powerful high sorceress, could transform into her human form and flee or murder Few Hairs, but spite runs hot in a spider's veins. Instead, she makes her way to Few Hairs' lips, where she wriggles herself into his mouth and down his throat.

The Grand Healer of Bon Chevalier bursts into lucidity, sitting up and scrambling for breath. He feels a tickling in his chest. *Must be the dust from the collapsed hut,* he thinks to himself.

"Bubbles! What have I done?" he gasps.

Few Hairs stumbles to his feet and limps out of the ruins. He discovers that his guards have been devoured by unholy roots. Their snails are missing, too.

Wait. He spots a shell amongst the thicket up ahead, slithering back and forth without direction.

"There is hope yet," he says, as if someone is listening, and heads toward the remaining snail.

* * *

Little Lady Alesing turns away from her crystal balls as the image of Power, Greed, and Beetroot shakes and cuts out.

What could have happened? she wonders.

"Guard!" A fearsome ogre adorned in iron armour enters. "I've received word that my younger brother and a band of thieves are here. Lock down the castle and find them."

"Wh-e-n th-ey 're foo-nd?" the ogre manages, still learning English.

"Don't…" She breathes. "Don't kill them. Bring them to me," she commands. The ogre nods and leaves her bedchambers.

Alesing heads to the throne room. She takes her throne. The Holy Stein O' Kin Beer sits on its podium.

CHAPTER 19

Feeling electric—not in the excited or adrenaline-filled way, but as if a pair of electrodes have been strapped to his balls—Bubbles steps over the dead ogres that line the wall and heads for the tower. Hops trips over himself, eager to follow, whilst the others dutifully fall behind.

A leader—He's a real leader, Hops sighs to himself. *But I'll show that I'm fit to be the grand lord. That Alesing is Wrong!*

The gang enters the tower and carefully sneak down the long, steep stairs. Bubbles watches the wall lamps light up the grey stones as they flicker. There's something introspective about fire, the way it elegantly dances, yet can so easily destroy. Of course, this thought doesn't pass through Ser Bubbles' head—it's far too deep. Instead, he wonders *if the magic flames in the throne room could melt my helmet off. Then I could enjoy a proper pint after all this.*

"What are ya doing, Bubbles?" Wimpy William asks, ogling his face.

"What?" Bubbles notices himself incessantly licking his lips in imagined pleasure. "Oh, urmm. Nevermind."

At the bottom of the steps, the gang are presented with an ajar door to their left and a hallway leading to the dungeons ahead of them.

"Which way, old chaps?" Lord Aaron asks.

"This door leads to the courtyard. From there, there's a hallway that leads to the throne room and a staircase that leads to the galleries," Bubbles explains.

"She's created many ogres, Brother. There's no way we can get to Alesing and The Stein without being swarmed. Certainly not with this many of us," Hops warns.

"Well, Brother, she kept you alive, didn't she?"

Hops nods, wondering where this is going.

"We don't all need to confront her. These thieves," he gestures to Wimpy William, Lord Aaron, and Brave Boros, "as ragtag as they may appear, are a skilled bunch."

The thieves nod their approval, though Boros offers more of an approving grunt.

Bubbles continues, "Only you and I, Brother Hops, must confront Alesing. Our friends here will focus on retrieving The Stein."

"Hate to put a damper on this hopeful moment, but how might we do that? You've not fully revealed your plan, Ser Bubbles," Lord Aaron interjects.

"Well, you were right, Lord Aaron; I *was* making it up as I go along," Bubbles admits. "Until this moment, I was considering facing my sister alone."

"She 'as an army of ogres, lad, not even I, *The Dwarf Who Grew—*" He winks. "—could face her alone."

"Do you really want to put your life on the line in exchange for beer?" Bubbles wonders.

"We're in too deep now, lad." William shrugs.

"And I've gained a taste for ogre blood," Boros jokes.

Bubbles looks last to Lord Aaron, who says, "I'm a lord without a home. Perhaps Beer can offer me one."

"Of course," Bubbles gleams. "Thank you, gentlemen. The beer will flow when all is said and done."

"Now, Brother," says Hops, "you were saying…"

"Ah, yes. You and I, Hops, will confront Alesing head-on. She's less likely to murder us in cold blood."

"Like she did Father."

"Yes, like she did Father. Meanwhile, Lord Aaron, Wimpy William, and Brave Boros will sneak into the throne room galleries and, using Aaron's rope, lower William behind Alesing's back where he can retrieve The Stein," Bubbles explains.

"Me again!" William complains.

"I'm afraid so. The alternative is that we all rush Alesing, but she won't think twice about killing you, William."

"And what of me?" asks Boros.

"I'm going to need someone to help hold the rope," Lord Aaron quips, looking at William's belly.

William clips Aaron on the knee.

"We'll need you to provide aerial support, Boros. I'm sure there'll be ogres guarding Alesing and The Stein," Bubbles says. "Now, first things first, we've got to get across the courtyard."

Bubbles peers around the ajar door and spots three ogres at the far end of the courtyard looking toward them, along with sentries wandering the above walls.

"They know we're here. They've replaced the sentries," Bubbles, gulps.

"And I suppose you want me t' take them out again," Boros wonders.

"No. It's better if we stay out of sight," Bubbles says.

"Maybe…" For the first time ever, with the confidence of those around him, Hops formulates an idea. "Boros, if you could take out one of the ogres at the far end, it could be enough to distract the other two. Bubbles and I could rush them from behind and take them out quietly. Then we could all run to the hallway entrance across the courtyard. I don't expect those sentries can see much down here, not under cover of night. Besides, they'll be focused on outside the castle walls."

Bubbles pats his brother on the shoulder approvingly. "Sounds like a plan."

"Shove over then." Boros moves to the open side of the door. Through the gap, he draws his bow and arrow, aiming at the farthest ogre. He looks down his sight, steadies his breath, and releases his fingers. The enchanted arrow zips through the air, buzzing past the skin of the other two ogres and pokes a hole through its target's head—the beast lands with a great thump, piquing the attention of the others.

"B-a-r-ry?" one ogre grunts.

"W-hy did-n't yoo moo-ve out the wa-y of this th-ing?" The other snaps the arrow out of his friend's head to examine its blackened tip.

Bubbles and Hops watch, hesitating at the sight of the curiously dumb beasts.

"Well, get to it," Boros remarks.

With the ogres hunched over their dead colleague, Ser Bubbles and Ser Hops of Beer draw their weapons, push open the door, and tacitly run to the end of the courtyard. Before the beasts have a chance to turn and realise what's happening, Bubbles' sword slices one's back and Hops' dagger opens the other's neck. They slump to the floor, leaking blood.

Staying in the shadows, the brothers creep to the hallway entrance on the other side of the courtyard. The thieves follow.

Whilst Lord Aaron, Brave Boros, and Wimpy William sing the brothers' praise as they stand in the hallway, Bubbles and Hops look at one another solemnly. *Who did they just kill,* they wonder. *The baker's son? The blacksmith? The stableboys?*

"Where's the throne room then?" Lord Aaron asks, breaking the brothers' glare.

"Just at the end of this corridor. To the left of the throne room doors, you'll find a staircase. Go up, and you'll reach the galleries," Bubbles explains.

The gang make haste down the corridor, where they find two ogres guarding the throne room door—they're swiftly met with an axe to the head and a sword to the belly.

"Good luck, old chaps." Lord Aaron nods, as do the others.

"You too." Bubbles regards the thieves for a moment—an impoverished bunch, each with a bad attitude of their own, but a bloody expert crew nonetheless. "Thank you all."

Bubbles and Hops awkwardly embrace before pushing the throne room doors open whilst the others head for the galleries.

CHAPTER 20

After dashing through the Definitely Evil Forest, Grand Healer Few Hairs finds his way to The Bastion of Beer, adrenaline keeping him going. He rides his snail like a racehorse, whipping and encouraging it to go faster and faster. Of course, slipping along the earlier slime tracks he and his guards snails earlier made makes this journey much swifter.

Few Hairs rides into Beer's village as the stars hang heavy above. He stops outside the tavern in which he and Bubbles previously met and dismounts from his snail. The healer gazes at the castle ahead—now it's Few Hairs' turn to find a way inside.

Not having the benefit of a band of thieves, professionals in the art of burglary, Few Hairs rubs his chin, considering bursting through the front doors on snailback.

Too risky, he thinks to himself. *If only I could somehow scale the wall, but I don't have a rope.*

Few Hairs looks at his snail in ponderance. It mews at him, twitching an eyelid.

Snails stick to things; why not a wall? he thinks. *But a giant snail, surely not. I'd be spotted immediately.*

Whether still dazed from the destruction of the witches' hut or thanks simply to a lack of options, Few Hairs considers that *he* was earlier transformed into a garden snail. *Perhaps I don't need a snail to scale the castle walls. Perhaps I can become the snail…*

Seemingly his only choice, Few Hairs leaves his snail hitched outside the tavern and heads to the front of the castle. He keeps low to avoid detection from the sentries at the top of the wall. He bounds toward the base of the wall, looking up at its vast height and stoney exterior.

That's a long way for a garden snail, he realises.

Nevertheless, Few Hairs flaps his hands in the air as if voguing and mutters a quiet spell to himself, *"Moi be escargot, moi be escargot, moi be escargot."*

With a burst of magical light, a spark in the air, and a manipulation of all physical possibilities, Few Hairs disappears. What remains is a garden snail navigating the uncut at the bottom of the wall.

For Beer! Few Hairs bravely whispers to himself as he creeps onto the wall with a sticky ripping sound.

Being completely vertical, it would not be a good time to get vertigo…or look down, as Few Hairs climbs higher. Alas, a snail's long eye is a wondering limb, almost with a mind of its own. So, as one eye looks forward, regarding the top of the wall, the other looks backwards, noticing the growing drop beneath.

Fortunately, Few Hairs is not afraid of heights—besides, taking a step back would reveal that he's not actually more than four feet off the ground—but the baby crow's head sticking out of a deep crack in the wall up ahead *is* concerning.

However, the great benefit of writing a fantasy novel is that if you need a narrative scapegoat, you can leverage the fictitious power of magic, saving you from in-depth planning and logic. This, dear reader, is one of those moments; because as Few Hairs considers how to avoid the ahead crow and get to the top of the wall swiftly, he remembers something immeasurably important: *he's magic.*

With this thought, Few Hairs clacks his eyes together like a pair of castanets and mumbles a ye olde spell. *Escargot go vite maintenant.*

His rear end begins to purr like a finely-tuned Harley Davidson motorcycle, and his teeth chatter like a vibrating engine. The trouble with this spell, Few Hairs, recalls, is that it has a tendency to fry snails from the inside out, so it's scarcely used by Bon Chevalierian healers. Still, Few Hairs puts confidence in his ability to reach the top before growing too hot. After all, he needs to hurry up.

Gritting his teeth, Few Hairs pings off at much more than a snails-pace, darting over bumps, cracks, and loose stones. He leaves the baby crow in the dust, singeing its feathers as he flies by.

Like hot coals, Few Hairs' eyes glow, heat lines emanate from his shell whilst smoke bellows from his bottom.

The top of the wall looms close, but so does melting point. If you've ever seen a snail fry from the inside out, which you likely haven't, you'll know that it looks like scrambled egg bursting out of a shell and bubbling in scorching oil.

Few Hairs feels his belly bubble with heat, but stopping now would cause too much friction—he'd likely explode; an ogre would see his remains and try to remember when and where it last sneezed. The only way to cool down and get over the wall is to keep going. He can use the wind to chill his rising temperature.

As Few Hairs approaches the top, he is catapulted into the air. He curves through the sky, his temperature stabilising as the wind rushes over his shell. His nose dives past the parapet to the other side of the wall.

Pop.

By mere inches, Few Hairs is able to stick to the wall, his eyes drooping downwards. He breathes a sigh of relief and lets gravity do the heavy lifting as he heads toward the courtyard and toward Bubbles.

CHAPTER 21

The throne room doors clip Hops on the arse as they slam shut behind him and Ser Bubbles. On the throne ahead of them sits their sister, her eyes ablaze with rage and her hair floating with magic. She is surrounded by a mighty guard of Ogres standing in a triangular formation. Together, their stench is almost unbearable, enough to make the brothers consider turning back.

"Brothers. Have you come to join my army?" Alesing snarls from across the room.

"Alesing. Look what you have become," Bubbles implores. "This isn't you."

Grand Lady Alesing casually steps down from the throne, caressing The Holy Stein O' Kin as she wanders on by. Her guards split, letting her pass through the middle.

"Oh, dear Brother, you are wrong. Too long have I been forced to take a back seat, never to be given the respect I deserve," she says coolly.

Bubbles takes a step forward. Immediately Alesings guard of ogres draws their swords, creating a cold metallic echo that radiates through the room.

"Sister. You are wrong. Father loved you dearly, he always spoke of what an excellent ruler you'd make," Bubbles pleads.

"Yes…If I had a cock!" she growls.

Hops looks to Bubbles. "It's no use, Brother. She has succumbed to sorcery."

"Dearest Hops. This is your doing. You could have stepped aside, as could have you, Bubbles, and Father would have had no choice but to pass his legacy to me. Yet, even in your weakness, you still aspired to rule Beer," Alesing says.

"It is my rite to rule, sister. I am first born," Hops bites. Bubbles shoots him daggers as Hops raises his.

"And what do you expect to do with that puny blade, Brother Hops?" she laughs. "Kill me?" Alesing turns away from her brothers and snaps her fingers as she takes her seat on the throne. "Seize them."

The ogres move forward as one—a disciplined band of soldiers loyally protecting their queen. Bubbles unsheathes his sword and takes a fighting stance, but before he or Hops make a move, arrows rain down from the above gallery to the left. Until now, Alesing hadn't noticed the thieves lurking above. Her mouth twitches with surprise.

One by one, the ogres fall as enchanted arrows pierce their heads.

"You dare kill my ogres!" Alesing booms. "These were once fine men of Beer. Their deaths should sit heavily on your conscience."

She is right, Bubbles thinks to himself. *We are murderers, but what else are we to do? Let Beer fall further into disarray?*

To her two remaining guards, Alesing commands, "Kill them!"

Hops is right. She truly is lost, Bubbles admits to himself as he clashes swords with an ogre. To Alesing's disappointment, Bubbles takes care of the beast with the skill of an experienced warrior, striking him down without a scratch to his armour. Hops, on the other hand, finds himself pinned to the floor by the mammoth weight of an ogre's belly. He frantically stabs his dagger into the beast's side, but it won't relent. Only when one of Boros' arrows finds itself embedded in the ogre's neck does Hops free himself.

"Your beasts are no match for us," Hops announces as he brushes himself off.

"Yes, I see you have friends," Alesing observes as she steps down from the throne. "But are you a match for me?"

Bubbles looks up to the gallery and spots Boros readying an arrow. He catches his eye and shakes his head. Boros disappointedly lowers his bow.

"So naïve, Brother. How's that helmet of yours, anyway?" she teases.

"It was you!" Bubbles shouts. "You're the reason I can't enjoy a refreshing pint, and why I had to sweat my way through the dessert!"

"I was hoping to leave you for dead in that desert, but those irksome Bon Chevalarians are a meddling bunch," she admits, stepping closer to her brother's and away from The Stein's podium, as blue fireballs ignite in her palms.

* * *

Hanging over the gallery banister overlooking the throne room, Brave Boros leans back, turning to Wimpy William and Lord Aaron. "It's time. She's away from The Stein."

Lord Aaron checks the rope tied around William's waist, ensuring it's tight enough. "Ready, William?"

"I hate being a dwarf!" he snaps as he pulls himself atop the banister and launches himself over the edge. Aaron and Boros watch, mouths agape, as William smacks into the side of a low-hanging wooden support beam. His belly slides down the side as he flails his arms and, by the skin of his teeth, manages to grasp onto the top of the beam.

Distracted by Grand Lady Alesing, Bubbles and Hops fail to notice the stumpy dwarf legs frantically kicking in the air as William struggles to pull himself atop the beam.

Meanwhile, Lord Aaron and Brave Boros grab hold of the other end of the rope and brace themselves to catch William's weight.

The dwarf stands on the other side of the beam, extends his arms like a bird, and slowly leans forward, putting all his faith in his clumsy companions.

He tips over the edge.

The rope slips through Aaron's and Boros' hands.

Wimpy William falls.

He keeps falling.

Snap.

Aaron and Boros catch the rope, stopping William from crashing onto the floor. He hangs awkwardly spinning in mid-air, a tall human length away from The Stein.

Beads of sweat drip from Boros' face as he braces behind Aaron, who grunts under the weight of William.

The pair cautiously release tiny lengths of the rope, inching the dwarf toward The Stein.

A groan bellows beside the pair.

They look to see an ogre rushing toward them, its sword raised.

Boros dives at the beast.

Lord Aaron slips forward and wedges his feet against the bottom of the banister to stop from slipping further and William falling.

Wimpy William jolts lower and starts to swing back and forth uncontrollably whilst Boros wrestles with the beast.

* * *

Embers swipe past Bubbles' helmet, and Hops ducks behind him.

"Sister, your curse is a blessing. That'd have scorched my curly locks if not for my helmet," Bubbles taunts.

A snarl rests on Alesing's face as she launches forward, nearly flying, toward Bubbles and Hops whilst angrily throwing fireballs. Bubbles dodges each shot, watching them magically evaporate into smoke. Hops, on the other hand, handles the coming projectiles with less tact. He stumbles and trips; yet, except for a few singed holes in his robes, he dodges the fire.

"You're no match for us, sister. Together we are strong. Please, surrender, and we will find a way to solve this amicably," Hops suggests naively.

"Spoken like the true ruler of Beer, Hops," says Bubbles.

At this, Alesing's face is awash with fury, but before she can muster up a fireball big enough to strike her brothers, the throne room doors fly open with a calamitous *bang*. They look round to see an insignificant garden snail waiting in the doorway.

With Alesing's attention taken by this strange sight, Bubbles and Hops edge behind her and seize her arms. She tries desperately to shake them off, but the brothers refuse to relent. And as her feet begin to leave the floor, using her dark sorcery to levitate, the snail erupts into a blue light. At that moment, an ogre corpse comes crashing down from the galleries with an arrow jammed in its eye. William, still swinging back and forth behind them, starts to become steady.

In front of Bubbles, Hops, and Alesing stands the Grand Healer of Bon Chevalier, transformed from snail to man.

"Kill that woman!" he booms, sword in hand.

Few Hairs raises his sword and lunges toward Alesing.

"Wait!" Bubbles shouts, but before Few Hairs can get anywhere near Alesing, he abruptly stops in his tracks.

"Healer?" Bubbles prompts whilst Hops and Alesing look on, confused.

Few Hairs' sword slips from his hand, locked in an arthritic spasm. His jaw, too, jaggedly opens and closes, swinging from side to side. He lets out a whimper and falls to his knees, his head bowed.

"Um...Sir?" Hops says timidly.

The healer brings his head up. The siblings recoil in horror as eight dark eyes emerge from Few Hairs' face, and fangs burst out of his mouth. His body contorts inhumanly and his skin peels away from his muscles.

Few Hairs slumps over. Is he dead?

Bubbles steps forward to investigate.

"Few Hairs?"

His corpse suddenly rips apart and explodes into a massive black mass of eight hairy legs, a bulging gut sack, and a nasty eight-eyed face.

"The Stein is mine!" the spider bellows.

* * *

Up in the galleries, Boros and Lord Aaron turn pale at the events below.

"Aaron, keep hold of William," Boros says.

Lord Aaron digs his feet beneath the banister, and Boros pulls out his bow. "My last arrow," he says, pulling it from its quiver. He looks below, aiming at the spider who blocks his view of Bubbles, Hops, and Alesing.

Steadying his breath, Brave Boros tracks the spider's gut sack, readying an arrow in his bow. A bead of sweat drips down his face. He releases the arrow.

As the arrow flies through the air, for a moment, it looks as though he's hit his mark. But out of nowhere, the spider flies up, sticking to the corner of the ceiling and spewing out a thick web that wraps up William, leaving him dangling from the rafters. The Stein, too, is suspended in the air by the spider's cloud-like web.

Boros watches in amazement, realising the trajectory of his arrow.

"Fuck!" he murmurs, his breath and blood draining from his body as he looks down and sees his arrow poking out of Alesing's chest.

"Sister!" Bubbles cries as the floor beneath him pools with blood. Alesing slumps in her brother's arms.

"Hops, take her to her bedchamber," Bubbles commands, tears welling in his eyes. "See that she lives."

Hops nods, mute from shock and fear. He and Alesing frantically stumble out of the room.

"Quickly!" Bubbles shouts, pain in his voice. He looks to Boros in the gallery, holding back a hateful cry. Boros hangs his head, showing his remorse.

CHAPTER 22

With his arms under her armpits, Ser Hops pulls Alesing to her bedchamber, struggling under her limp weight. A line of blood follows them, tramlined by Alesing's droopy heels.

"Brother…" she weakly mumbles.

"We'll get you fixed up, Alesing, just hang in here," Hops says as he lifts her onto the bed, her body weakly slumping.

"Brother…" Alesing murmurs again, her eyes flickering.

"Is Grand Healer Trappy an ogre?" Hops asks.

Alesing coughs in response. Her head falls to the side.

"Of course he is..." Hops mutters to himself, surveying his sister and the room. "Let's see here…" He reaches toward the arrow still protruding from Alesing's chest and grasps its shaft. She lets out a wild wail like a ghoul haunting its tormentor. Hops quickly retracts his hand.

"I'm sorry, sister. This is going to hurt, but I need to get that arrow out," Hops say remorsefully, as his sister's blood soaks into the bed sheets. He grips the arrow and yanks it out in one swift movement—his hand turns red with blood. Alesing lets out a quiet whimper before her face turns pale, her eyes close, and her murmurs go quiet.

"Sister?" Hops throws the arrow aside.
"Sister?" He frantically shakes her shoulders, trying to wake her. "No…" Hops kneels beside her bed, his head in his hands.

"Brother…" Alesing gasps, returning to a conscious state. She claws at her chest wound, dazed. "What's going on?"

"Alesing," he sighs. "You've been shot with an arrow." Hops uses his dagger to cut a long strip of fabric from the bed sheets.

"Here," he says. "Let me wrap your wound."

As Hops wraps Alesing's wound, she grunts and gasps and tsks in pain, but through it, she manages to speak, "Brother, the things I've done…"

"Hush now, sister. I must finish wrapping you." And so he does.

"I was…blinded," Alesing says.

"Blinded?"

"I was blinded…by anger."

"Your mind was poisoned by those sorcerers."

"It was I who called upon them, Brother."

"Why, Alesing?"

"I wanted to be the first grand lady of Beer—" she wheezes, "—but Father would never allow it."

"Sister, I'd have made you my chief advisor. I'd have listened to your wisdom. You'd have been given the highest honour any woman can have. You would not be disregarded. And now, because of all you've done, I must rule Beer without you." Hops looks down, watching his sister's blood trickle along the floorboards.

"I never wanted to rule Beer with you, Brother. I wanted to rule alone," she rasps. "You're too weak to rule."

"You're wrong!" Hops snaps. "I just don't want power or fame, like you. I want peace and harmony."

"Power keeps your enemies in line, Brother. It keeps the people safe."

"Is that what you were doing, was it? Keeping the people safe," Hops morbidly chuckles. "You lost everything for greed and power, sister."

"It *is* my rite to rule Beer. I am the eldest, whether I've got a cock between my legs or not." She coughs and sputters. Hops adjusts her pillows. "But…perhaps, you're right," submission hangs in her voice. "Perhaps I didn't do this the right way. Perhaps there was a peaceful solution."

"You succumb to the Cup 'n' Sorcerers' influence, sister. It's easily done," Hops admits.

Alesing brings a weak hand to Hops' face. "You were always my favourite, you know?"

Hops ruefully smiles.

"Promise me something, Brother." Her hand drops to the bed. "Promise me that you will bring about a change—that I do not die in vain."

Holding her cold hand, Hops nods, considering to himself whether her death should be in vain after the pain she's caused. He doesn't tell her this—now is not the moment, because as Hops regards his sister, her eyes slowly close for the last time. Her breath leaves her body and her chest grows still.

Hops hunches over and presses his forehead to his sister's hand. He sobs a sorrowful cry, and the darkened night sky begins to turn orange with the morning sun. A new day is upon Beer.

CHAPTER 23

As the spider hisses in the corner of the ceiling, its legs bent, ready to lunge, Brave Boros and Lord Aaron haul themselves over the gallery banister, slipping down to join Ser Bubbles.

"I need a sword! I'm out of arrows," Boros announces. "Don't need an enchanted weapon to kill a spider, old chap. Take one from a corpse," Lord Aaron suggests.

The spider darts down in front of Bubbles and rears its fearsome fangs. "Little help here, lads!" Bubbles shouts to the thieves as he backs away from the arachnid's advances.

"Just a second, Bubbles," Boros says as Lord Aaron joins the fight. Boros hunches over an ogre corpse and shimmies its sword out from its giant green hands. Only, he notices that as he does so, the hand appears to shrink and flash from the colour of bogies to the beige colour of skin. The beast's bulldozer knuckles transform into unimpressive bumps and its sickly face shirks its bloated structure. Most fascinatingly to Boros, the would-be beast's stench of garlic dissipates, replaced by the ever-so-slightly less sour scent of death. Boros looks around. The other corpses—they, too, have lost their monstrous build, returning to who they once were.

"Um…" Boros stutters. "Bubbles, do you know what's happening 'ere?"

Just having landed from a backwards lunge, Bubbles ducks, narrowly avoiding a swipe from the spider's hairy leg, whilst Lord Aaron tumbles backwards, swinging his sword aimlessly in the spider's direction. Bubbles looks over to Boros, where he spots the corpse.

It's human… he thinks to himself.

As the spider snarls and erratically attacks him and Aaron, for a moment, Bubbles zones out, switching to auto-pilot as he defensively dodges the spider. He looks around the room, taking note of the corpses.

But that means... he realises what's happened. *Alesing...Sister...No!*

"She's dead!" Bubbles cries, snapping back into reality as a spider leg comes bounding toward his face.

Smack!

He goes flying backwards.

At this sight, Lord Aaron gets a grip of himself and stands in a sturdy fighting position, his sword poised forward. As the spider approaches him, it stops to consider the pompous thief, who swings his weapon through the air toward the arachnid's leg. It's stopped by a gloopy web before it can make contact.

"And who might you be?" the spider cackles.

"I'm—I'm Lord Aaron of Cawk," he says bravely.

The spider bellows a laugh. "Well, Lord Aaron of Cawk, I'm rather hungry, and you look a tasty meal."

His eyes widen at the prospect of being eaten by a giant spider—it's not the death he'd imagined. In fact, Lord Aaron would very much like to die watching the busty topless women of Bon Chevalier press grapes with their feet, perhaps from over-excitement. But that doesn't look likely as the spider sneakily wraps its web up Aaron's arm with a menacing sneer on its face.

Luckily for Lord Aaron, Brave Boros has stopped ogling the transforming corpses in bewilderment and flies into the spider's side with his sword.

The arachnid jolts back, releasing its web with a piercing high-pitched yowl.

Lord Aaron pulls the web off his sword and arm.

"You all right there, bruvva?" Boros asks. "You look a little green around t' gills."

Behind them, Bubbles pulls himself to his feet, shaking off the blow to his head.

This helmet...I'd be dead if not for Alesing's magic, he admits to himself. *Surely though...if she's dead.*

Bubbles dares to grasp the base of his golden helmet with two hands and pull hopefully upwards. It twists and budges but won't quite come off all the way.

Damn, he thinks. *But she's dead...*

"Stop fucking 'bout with your helmet an' come 'elp us!" Boros interrupts.

Ser Bubbles jumps to his feet and joins the thieves. The three of them stand in a line opposite the spider, with Wimpy William still hanging above. They shake their heads, stomp their boots, and ready themselves for the spider to attack.

Bubbles has an idea, which despite the urgent nature of the situation, he feels he has time to discuss.

"Boros," he says out of the corner of his mouth. "We'll distract the spider; you grab some arrows from the corpses. When I say the word, shoot William down."

"I'll bang me 'ead!" the dwarf grumbles from above.

"Yes, but not on the floor," Lord Aaron quips, realising Bubbles' plan.

"Go for the gut sack," Bubbles instructs.

"The gut…" William lets out a sigh. "I better be paid well for this, I'm telling ya," he shivers.

How the spider didn't hear this conversation is a miracle of fictional storytelling. Nevertheless, the arachnid bounds toward our heroes like a bull raging at the colour red.

Boros lunges left towards a, now human, corpse whilst Bubbles and Lord Aaron dive right, letting the spider fly past them. Mid-jump, the spider bears its fangs, but it misses its target and clasps down on the throne—it lets out a painful shriek as its teeth bend backwards on the glass.

Bubbles looks over to Boros as he yanks two arrows from a cadaver and loads them into his quiver. The spider's eight eyes crawl toward Boros, watching him ready his weapon. It stomps around, leaning on its back legs, ready to lunge toward Boros, but before it's able to leap, it notices its back end tilting sideways.

"My…" the arachnid roars in agony, unable to finish its sentence. Lord Aaron stands behind the spider, panting, whilst his sword drips with blood, and a severed spider leg lies discarded before him.

In what seems like an instant, the spider flickers from Boros' face to Bubbles' and Lord Aaron's, who stand confronted by its fury. However, reliving their unease

A FANTASY NOVEL THAT GETS STRAIGHT TO THE POINT

(just a little as no ill feeling can be truly relieved when there's an abnormally large arachnid starring you in the face—consider that terrified feeling that creeps up your spine when you find a spider sharing your shower, now imagine that spider is responsible for possessing your elder sister's soul) is Wimpy William kicking his legs above.

Zeal rushes back into Bubbles' face as he notices the dwarf above and the spider's position below. In their scuffle, Bubbles and Lord Arron push the arachnid back, right under William's unhappy half-sized kickers.

"Boros!" Bubbles gulps. "Now!"

The spider's eyes dart around, confused as to the meaning of Bubbles' signal. At the same time, Boros expertly loads an arrow into his bow and takes aim at the web suspending William. He releases the arrow. It shoots through the air, hits the spider's web and tears it apart. Wimpy William drops and lands on the spider with a soft thud. He mounts the arachnid, like an eight-legged horse, holding on to a clump of its head hair.

"She's a wriggler," William shouts as the spider tries to buck him off. *A wriggler...* William remembers that he's mounted on a spider, not a horse. He shudders.

"William," Bubbles shouts. "The gut sack!"

The others back away from the erratically kicking arachnid, their weapons still raised. William raises his axe and mashes it into the spider. It lets out an enraged wail and bucks even harder—William flies up, his rear leaving the spider, but he remains mounted thanks to his tight grasps on the spider's hair. The gut sack starts to split, but its thick skin keeps it pulled together.

As the arachnid bucks wonkily around the room, Bubbles and Lord Arron poke their swords at its legs, trying to keep it under control to stop William from falling off. He bashes the spider's gut sack again. The spider kicks its remaining legs. Again—*Whack!* The arachnid's legs give way, and its belly presses to the floor. As it lays helplessly, William raises his axe for one final blow. The spider eyes Bubbles, whispering with menace, "This is not the end, Ser Bubbles."

Splat.

The spider's gut sack bursts open. Blood and entrails ooze out, washing the floor a lurid yellow colour.

Ser Bubbles of Beer, Lord Aaron of Cawk, Brave Boros, and Wimpy William lower their weapons to their sides and catch their breath as they soak up the scene, the dwarf standing in a pool of guts.

"The Stein." Bubbles remembers, looking up at the relic still suspended in mid-air. "It must be destroyed. This can't happen again."

"Ser Bubbles…" a weak voice croaks from the doorway. Bubbles turns to see the Grand Healer of Beer. "Trappy, you're still alive," he says in awe.

"Yes. Though it's as if I just woke up from a long sleep, and my hands smell of onions," the healer explains. He looks around the room, taking in the unusual scene. "What's happened, my lord?"

"How much do you remember before your transformation?" Bubbles asks.

"Only your sister losing her mind," the healer replies.

"That's about the size of it. Any recommendations on destroying The Stein?" Bubbles wonders.

"Well, you could throw it in the flames of The MoTowntain, but…"

"A band of thieves, one of whom is a dwarf, and a powerful relic that needs to be destroyed by throwing it into a volcano…sounds too familiar," Bubbles notes.

"Yes. Quite." Grand Healer Trappy strokes his chin in thought. "Best smash it to pieces then."

"William?" Bubbles asks.

Wimpy William lobs his axe at The Stein. It flies through the air in slow motion.

Smash.

A million shards of glass shatter through the air, glistening in the light. It rains down like confetti—signifying a job well done. Of course, it *is* glass, which isn't something you want raining down like confetti. So, the group turn their backs to the ceiling and cover their faces to avoid being struck by sharp shards.

"There ye go, Ser Bubbles," Williams says, rising. "Now, where's mah ale?"

CHAPTER 24

Ser Bubbles, Ser Hops, the three thieves, and the Grand Healer of Beer slink into their chairs around a table in the feasting hall, steins of Beer's Best Beer in front of them. Still catching their breath from the earlier confrontation, they leave their drinks to settle for a moment. The beer foam pops and crackles, looking oh-so refreshing.

As they sit, their chests heavily rising and falling, Lord Aaron breaks the silence by raising his stein triumphantly. "A toast," he says. "To defeating that wretched spider."

The others raise their glasses and clink them together. Each of them take a generous sip of beer, apart from Bubbles who places his stein back down on the table, untouched. He looks at it wishfully and suppresses a resigned sigh.

"And to…" Hops pipes up. "To my sister, Alesing."

"Yer sister?" William's face drops. "She caused all o' this mess."

Hops stares daggers at Brave Boros, who nudges William apologetically.

"To Alesing," Boros says, raising a glass.

They clink their glasses, Bubbles again not sipping his beer.

"You know," Boros starts. "I di'n't mean to…"

"It's not your fault Boros," Bubbles interrupts forgivingly. He looks down at his beer, fiddling with the glass. The room falls quiet.

"Ser Hops, it's time we organise your coronation," the Grand Healer of Beer politely cuts the atmosphere. "The people have been through a traumatic experience. They need a leader."

Ser Hops looks down at his hands. "I'm not…" He glances around the table in the otherwise empty feasting hall. His brother Bubbles, Grand Healer Trappy, Wimpy

William, Brave Boros, and Lord Aaron of Cawk watch him intently. Bubbles nods his encouragement.

"The grand healer is right, Brother. It's time," Bubbles says, smiling beneath his helmet.

"It's strange. I can't help but miss her, even though she turned out to be evil," Hops says solemnly.

"She was our sister. For years she wasn't evil."

"My lord, it's time we coronated you," the grand healer places a reassuring hand on Hops' shoulder. "Your father would be proud."

Hope, joy, hatred, and upset flush across Hops' moist eyes at these words. After all, Alesing was always his father's favourite.

"You know, Hops. I mean, my lord," Lord Aaron fumbles his words with a wink. "Seeing as Bon Chevalier is no longer in need of my family's services, might I request that we kindly provide you and yours with beer bottle stoppers? For the coronation, at least. It would be an honourable reward."

"Hold on!" William interrupts. "If he's getting his reward now, I want mine, too!"

"What do you wan'? A new step ladder?" Brave Boros snaps.

Wimpy William eyes Boros with a chasm of contempt.

"Why I oughta," he pulls his fist back like an enraged cartoon character.

Bubbles looks to Hops and laughs, absentmindedly trying to sip his beer.

Clonk.

Once again, his beer-guzzling is stifled by his blasted helmet.

"Healer," Bubbles says. "This helmet—Alesing cursed it to remain stuck on my head. Only, I expected the curse to break when she died. Yet, it still won't budge."

The Grand Healer of Beer examines Bubbles' helmet with interest. "Yes, I believe the curse should have been broken. Perhaps your head has expanded under the heat of the helmet."

"Or you've grown too big-headed, Brother," Hops jibes. "After all, you did save Beer."

"That's a possibility, Ser Bubbles," the healer says. "But you'd have to be pretty big-headed for it to get permanently stuck."

"Enough of your jibes," Bubbles barks. "How do I get it off?"

"A good hard tug," Trappy suggests.

"Filthy," Lord Aaron quips.

"It's pretty stuck. It'd need a lot of force," Bubbles says.

"How could we do this?" Lord Aaron wonders, once again eyeing Wimpy William.

"What now?" William grumbles.

* * *

As surrounding soldiers busy themselves with training in the courtyard, Ser Bubbles stands face to cheek with the back end of Wimpy William's levitating ass.

"Why couldn't we use a regular horse?" Bubbles asks whilst Lord Aaron finishes tying the end of a rope around his helmet.

"Well," Lord Aaron explains, "fall into the back of a horse and it'll kick you to death. This mule doesn't use its legs. Plus, it'll be a smooth pull, thanks to its levitation."

"Have you done this before?" Bubbles asks quizzically.

"Funnily enough," William shouts from beside his mule, fastening a knot around his animal, "we've been in a similar situation with a goblin, a rabbit, and a whore."

"Ah…" Bubbles lip twitches.

"Ready?" Lord Aaron smacks Bubbles on the back. He nods reluctantly.

"Go ahead, William." Aaron puts his thumb up to the dwarf whilst Brave Boros and Ser Hops look on with disbelief.

"One." William counts.

Boros cracks a smile.

"Two."

The dwarf stands stoutly whilst Lord Aaron looks on with amusement.

"Three."

Whack.

William slaps his mule's behind, causing it to screech and canter forward. Ser Bubbles' neck slowly extends, appearing elastic. He lets out a whimper, but his helmet doesn't budge.

"Stop," Bubbles shouts.

"Everything okay, Ser Bubbles?" Lord Aaron asks.

"Yes," he replies, trying to save face. "Just a little painful." He breathes deeply. "Try again."

The mule pulls once more, again to no avail. They try many more times until Ser Bubbles has gained a foot in height.

"No. This isn't working," Ser Bubbles determines.

"What do you suggest we do?" Lord Aaron inquires.

"Oh…I don't know," he sighs. "We'll give it one more try. Wimpy William, don't hold back this time."

"As you say."

With that, Wimpy William kicks his mule up a storm. Its legs flail, its tail flaps and it *honks* a horrible noise. Similarly, Ser Bubbles lets out an animalistic rumble and, with one great roar….

Pop.

Ser Bubbles' helmet flies off and tumbles through the air, splashing in a nearby water trough. But it's not just his helmet — the forward force, strong as it was, causes Ser Bubbles to lunge forward with the power of an Olympian, his head headed directly for the mule's arsehole.

Pop.

"Oh, dear," Lord Aaron remarks.

Boros looks over to Wimpy William and Ser Hops, who both champion faces like slapped *asses*. Their mouths open wide as they bellow and giggle.

The group hear Bubbles pleading for help, muffled by the mule's insides.

"Wimpy William, looks like you're going to need a new mule," quips Lord Aaron.

"What have yoo been doing t' that mule, William?" Boros asks. "It's barely flinched."

Wimpy Williams's face turns red. "What are ye suggesting?" He approaches Boros, shoulders squared.

"Nothing. Just that, if this mule weren't used t' this sort of thing, it'd probably jump, kick, and holler." He chuckles.

"Mhmhmhmhmh!" Bubbles interrupts, whatever that means.

"Gentlemen," Lord Aaron sighs. "Enough of this. We've a man's head that needs removing."

"How do we remove him?" asks Ser Boros.

"Boros, tie my stallion to Ser Bubbles' waist," Lord Aaron commands.

"Pull your pants down then."

"Flattery will get you nowhere, Boros."

Ser Boros tightly ties a rope around Ser Bubbles' waist and Lord Aaron's horse.

"Right-o. Ready, Ser Bubbles?" Lord Aaron asks.

"Mhmhmhmhmhm!" Ser Bubbles replies, distressed.

Whack. Lord Aaron slaps his stallion's backside, causing it to gallop forward with a mighty pull.

Pop.

"Ahhh," Ser Bubbles breathes heavily, "thank the gods!"

Remembering himself, Bubbles pats at his head, feeling, for the first time in days, not metal, but his wiry and curly hair (a bit of donkey shite, too). Then he notices a wet feeling on his ear.

What is that, he wonders.

Bubbles turns to see William's mule nibbling and licking his ear.

CHAPTER 25

A glorious day shines on The Bastion of Beer as the throne room fills with townsfolk and farmers. Its walls are adorned with long banners flying Beer's coat of arms—a clump of barely—and a long golden carpet stretching from the base of The Plastered Throne to the open doorway. To the left of the throne waits Grand Healer Trappy and Ser Bubbles, his black curly hair resting on his shoulders. To the right, Wimpy William stands tidily next to Lord Aaron, who dresses in his green robes of Cawk, whilst Brave Boros remains in his battle armour. They don't look too bad for a ragtag bunch.

The crowd whoop and bustle in their seats as the Grand Healer of Beer takes centre stage.

He speaks, hushing the crowd, "Ladies and gentlemen of Beer. We thank you for joining us on this momentous occasion. Now, please, all rise for Ser Hops, the Little Lord of Beer."

The grand healer steps to the side of the carpet as four horn players sound a regal tune from the corners of the room. The townsfolk quietly clamber to their feet, and everyone, from the galleries to the back of the throne room, watches the door with anticipation.

Ser Hops of Beer steps onto the carpet wearing a long flowing golden cape and his father's old coronation armour—a flaxen-coloured suit of chainmail that shimmers under the blue fire of the throne room.

As Ser Hops makes his way toward the healer, the townsfolk respectfully bow. Hops looks around at the eyes watching him. In the galleries, the people beam, and beside him, the townsfolk gawp in awe.

"Please," Hops says to a man bowing almost to his knees. "You may sit."

He turns to the crowd, "You all may sit. This is *our* day. This is *your* day."

Cautiously the townsfolk begin to sit, a puzzled expression on their faces.

"And enough with the horns!" Hops shouts. The brass instruments fall silent, as does the room.

Hops approaches the throne and kneels before the Grand Healer of Beer, who speaks, "Traditionally, I would present you with Beer's oldest relic, The Holy Stein O' Kin Beer, and have you swear on its sanctity. Due to recent events, that is not possible." He gestures to the empty podium sitting beside the throne. "Instead, you will swear on the empty podium where The Stein once sat, representing the absence of evil in Beer."

Ser Hops stands up and places his hand on the podium. He bows his head.

"Close your eyes and repeat after me," the grand healer says. Hops does so.

"I, Ser Hops of Beer, eldest son of the late Grand Lord Slosh, do solemnly swear to protect the people of Beer and its lands. Be there a day where darkness falls upon The

Bastion of Beer once again, I swear to take up arms without hesitation in the pursuit of the eradication of evil."

Grand Healer Trappy places a bejewelled crown on Hops' head.

"Open your eyes," Trappy says quietly. Then he booms, "Turn and address your people, Grand Lord Hops of Beer."

The people cheer and clap and whoop.

"You saved us, my lord!" an overjoyed peasant cries.

Hops opens his mouth to speak, and the room falls silent, "I did not save you alone. In fact, I only played a small part. It is these gentlemen behind me that are your true saviours. And as a thank you for saving my people, I would like to bestow gifts upon them."

The grand healer hands Grand Lord Hops a small wooden box. He approaches the free swords.

"The free swords known as Wimpy William and Brave Boros, you are without allegiances—without lands to call your own. For your service to the people of Beer, I gift you a field each, as much beer and ale as you can guzzle, and these—" Hops opens the box, revealing three golden shield-shaped badges emblazoned with the mark of Beer. "These are badges of honour and, if you agree to it, signify your service to Beer as part of my personal guard."

Hops turns to Lord Aaron of Cawk. "Though you already have a place in Cawk, there is a badge here for you too, Lord Aaron."

Lord Aaron takes the badge from the wooden box and regards it with astonishment.

"Where I come from, I'm a disappointment. My father treats me as no more than a salesman." He looks Hops in the eyes. "I would be honoured to serve as a member of your personal guard." In his theatrical demeanour, Lord Aaron falls to his knees, gushing in reverence.

"Do we need'a do that?" William quietly asks Boros, who shrugs.

"And you two—" Hops looks to William and Boros, who quickly straighten themselves up. "Do you accept?"

They enthusiastically nod, almost without hesitation.

"And finally, then. My younger brother." Hops approaches Bubbles. "You have always served as Beer's fiercest warrior. In fact, there have been many times in which I thought Father would name *you* his heir," he friendlily chuckles. "Now, I ask that you be my chief advisor and head of my personal guard."

Bubbles bows his head. "Of course, dear Brother." Grand Lord Hops places a hand on Bubbles' shoulder and smiles proudly at his brother. He then turns to the throne.

The throne, this is what it's all been about, Hops thinks to himself.

With a flourish of his cape, Hops takes his place on the throne as the *Grand Lord* of Beer. The crowd erupt with elation.

"One more thing!" Hops booms, quieting the crowd. "Tradition, though an important standard by which to hold ourselves, must not stifle the betterment of our people. So, in light of recent events, as my first act as Grand Lord of Beer, I declare that, from this day forth, first daughters will have just as much right to rule Beer as first sons."

The crowd collectively gasp and murmur to one another in both contempt and joy. Meanwhile, Hops looks out into his subjects and notices a little girl with big wet eyes tugging at her mother's robes. Unlike everyone else, the girl is silent. She looks up at Hops in awe.

CHAPTER 26

The castle hallways ring quiet. Golden streamers and confetti gently tumble along the floor where Beerian guards and a few townsfolk, still hanging on from the earlier feast, lay inebriated. Typically after such a raving party, you'd find Ser Bubbles and Grand Lord Hops passed out somewhere they shouldn't be—the stables, a lucky maiden's bed, or maybe ambling along the road to Clubland. Tonight, however, the brothers are in the local graveyard, just outside the village on a nearby hill, pensively watching their sister's coffin lowered into an unmarked grave under the glaring moonlight.

"Does it have to be unmarked, Healer?" asks Hops, looking at the grand healer who stands with them, his head bowed.

"She turned everyone into ogres, my lord. Her grave would be desecrated if the townsfolk knew its location," the healer explains.

"These men know." Hops looks at the undertakers with squinted eyes as they set Alesing's coffin into the ground.

"And these men will be paid handsomely for their troubles," Bubbles notes, nodding at the men.

"Leave us," Grand Healer Trappy says to the undertakers. The men respectfully bow to Grand Lord Hops and Ser Bubbles, then return to the nearby church.

"It might help, my lord, if you were to say some words," says the healer to Hops. "You too, Ser Bubbles." The brothers glance at one another uncertainly.

"I…" Hops trembles and speaks in a subdued voice. "I have honoured your last wishes, Sister. If I have a daughter first, she will take my place as Grand Lord of Beer when I pass. Rest peacefully, knowing your legacy is not that of dark sorcery."

Hops wipes his eyes and sniffles, "Brother, have you anything to say?"

Ser Bubbles steps closer to his sister's gave, considering her coffin. "*Bethison*," he says. "You murdered our father," his voice cracks. "You tortured our people with magic. And you got yourself killed in the process. *Bethison*, sister. Yet," he gulps, "I will always love you and value your wisdom."

Grand Lord Hops pats Bubbles on the back, "She would have made a fine ruler, Brother."

"Let us each say a silent prayer," the healer says. They bow their heads, close their eyes, and ask the gods—whoever they are, Jive Turkey?—to forgive Alesing. Alas, prayers tend to fall on deaf ears, and on this occasion, it's no different. For as Bubbles, Hops, and Trappy pray, something ungodly happens inside Alesing's coffin.

Her cadaver lies pale and ripe, and her mouth hangs agape, stiffly stuck and contorted. The undertakers made an effort to dress Alesing in her regal golden robes of Beer before placing her in her coffin, but her garments are now awash with darkness. Yet this darkness is just a lack of light.—it's crawling sea of wriggling black spiders leaking in from the cracks in the side of her wooden box. Hundreds of spiders and mini beasts hiss, creak, and clack.

"Can you…" Bubbles looks around, confused. "Can you hear that?"

"What?" asks Hops.

"That hiss like—" He puts his hand to his head. "—like a million voices suddenly crying out in terror."

"A disturbance in the force, you mean?" the healer suggests.

"Something like that, yes."

"No. Can't hear it," Hops says dismissively whilst the healer shakes his head.

Meanwhile, the army of spiders climb Alesing's body, making their way from the bottom of her legs to her head. One by one, the arachnids drop into her ajar mouth, filling up her insides. They flicker across the whites of her eyes and burst out of her ears. Alesing is undoubtedly dead, but her cadaver is very much still alive, bustling with bugs, the new home of the Cup 'n' Sorcerers.

A FANTASY NOVEL THAT GETS STRAIGHT TO THE POINT

Bubbles looks up from his sister's grave at Hops, "Pint?"

THANK YOU FOR READING.

IF YOU ENJOYED THIS BOOK, PLEASE LEAVE A POSITIVE REVIEW ON AMAZON.

Printed in Great Britain
by Amazon